Cli-Fi Plus

Treesong

Published by Cranncheol Publishing, 2020.

This book is dedicated to everyone who has taken action in response to anthropogenic global warming and to the future generations of human and non-human life who will inherit the world created by our choices.

Foreword

For the past decade or so, I've been an enthusiastic reader and writer of climate fiction (cli-fi). After completing and publishing my first cli-fi novel, Change, I took a break to gather my thoughts and get other aspects of my life together. When I returned to my writing, I decided to write cli-fi short stories for my Patreon account and occasionally for submission to magazines and contests.

At first, I didn't have a specific goal or theme in mind other than climate. I just wrote about whatever ideas came to me. The more I wrote, though, the more I started to view these stories as an ongoing exploration of the wide range of possibilities of cli-fi.

Cli-fi is an incredibly broad and versatile genre that is still discovering its voice and its place in the literary world. By definition, it always includes some significant reference to the climate. But it can also include just about any other narrative elements and genre tropes. This opens up countless possibilities—and many of them have yet to be explored.

Once I realized this, I decided to explore these possibilities, one story at a time. I was especially interested in writing crossover stories where elements of cli-fi were combined with elements of more established genres and subgenres. What would a cli-fi alien story look like? What would a cli-fi robot story look like? What would a cli-fi zombie story look like? What would a cli-fi time travel story look like? With these questions in mind, I decided to write a series of short stories that explored the intersections between climate change and non-climate genres and narrative themes.

This anthology is the culmination of that effort.

After considering many titles, I named this anthology "Cli-Fi Plus" for two reasons. The first is that some of these stories were initially inspired by the very simple idea of a crossover: "Cli-fi Plus" another genre or theme. The second is that my hope with this anthology, and my writing in general, is to enrich and expand our understanding of what cli-fi is and what it can accomplish. As authors and as critical readers, we're exploring new literary territory by expanding this genre from its simplistic post-apocalyptic roots into something more complex and rewarding. I would like to frame this emerging take on the scope and depth of climate fiction as Cli-Fi Plus.

Yes, the genre includes some stories of people who are displaced by flooding or similar climate catastrophes. These "climate disaster" stories are still important stories to tell, especially while people in the real world face the imminent threat and lived experience of such climate catastrophes. But the genre of climate fiction isn't limited to that narrow interpretation. There are so many more climate-related stories to tell—from tales of very personal and realistic struggles with the everyday consequences of climate change and climate policy, to the fantastic tales of aliens, robots, zombies, time travelers, and beyond.

In this anthology, I've organized these stories into three different sections.

Tales of What Might Be are stories that could very well take place in the near future. They contain some speculative elements such as the exact extent of the consequences of human-caused global warming and our responses to that warming. But they don't venture into anything too far removed from reality as we know it.

Tales from the Edge push the boundary between fact and fiction. They take place in a world that is still similar to our own, but human actions, or the consequences of those actions, or both, soon take us to the edge of what we know and what we believe to be possible.

Tales from Beyond are stories whose very premise is in some way speculative from the outset. This is where we find the time travelers, the aliens, the robots, and the zombies. There's nothing particularly new about telling stories that contain these speculative sci-fi elements. However, combining these elements with the theme of climate is fairly new—and it can take us to interesting new places.

This three-section framework is somewhat arbitrary. But personally, I found it to be a fun opportunity to reflect on the similarities and differences among a variety of climate narratives. It may also help some readers decide which climate stories they'd like to read first, or at all. Do you usually read "normal" fiction? "Weird" fiction? Something in-between? Wherever you fall on that spectrum, there's climate fiction there that you're sure to enjoy.

Human-caused climate change affects all aspects of our lives. Let's see how it affects all aspects of our literature. We're storytelling creatures, so even in the midst of a global climate crisis, we'll continue telling a vast, diverse, and seemingly endless collection of stories. Let's find out where climate fits into these stories. It will certainly provide us with some new and entertaining tales to read. And if we're lucky, at the end of the day, it may also help us to understand more about where the climate crisis and its solutions fit into our personal and collective stories.

Tales of What Might Be

"Every time I look at those IPCC charts, I envision what the world will be like in each emission scenario. I imagine what ordinary people's lives will be like if we follow that path."

Three Scenarios
Fill The Gap
Welcome to Synergy Central
Spread the Sunshine

Three Scenarios

Kandace and Abe staggered hand in hand through the entrance of the Emergency Department of the Hôtel-Dieu de Paris. When a nurse saw Abe's bleeding head and unsteady gait, she rushed toward him. Abe pushed her away, pointing at his wife's pregnant belly.

"Douleurs d'accouchment! L'enfant vient!"

When the nurse saw Kandace, she waved another nurse over to help. The four of them made their way across the lobby.

Abe squeezed Kandace's hand.

"We might have to go to separate rooms. I'm sorry."

Kandace frowned, squeezing Abe's hand with tears in her eyes.

"I know. Find me as soon as you can. And take care of yourself, okay?"

"I will, honey. I love you!"

"I love you, too!"

After a brief conversation in a mix of French and English, the nurses coaxed the couple into letting go of each other's hands. They waved goodbye as the nurses led them in separate directions.

Kandace was reclining in bed with her newborn in her arms. Her hospital gown was pulled down on one side so the baby could nurse at her breast. She felt sore and exhausted beyond words, but holding her baby filled her with an overwhelming sense of comfort.

Abe was curled up in a chair next to Kandace's bed. He was still a patient himself, but he had responded well to bandaging and rehydration, so the doctor had cleared him to visit Kandace. He laid his head against his chair and turned to look at his wife and child.

"I was worried about both of you. You're two weeks early! Was it the stress of the protest? Should we have stayed home?"

Kandace smiled. "It's sweet that you worried, but I'm fine. Little Ava is fine, too. I was worried about you! It just seemed scary because we were in the middle of a protest. Two weeks early isn't bad. The doctor said Ava didn't even seem early. She's a little light, but she has a healthy heart and lungs. It's as if she knew she'd be arriving early."

"Maybe she wanted to be born today. She must share her mother's passion for getting into trouble."

They both smiled. Abe placed his hand palm up on Kandace's lap. Kandace held the baby in one arm and reached out with the other to hold Abe's hand. They sat together in silence, holding hands and looking at their newborn.

Eventually, Kandace looked away with a sigh. She turned toward the window with a distant look in her eyes. Abe held her hand a little tighter to be sure that she wouldn't pull away like she sometimes did when she got that look.

"What's wrong, honey?"

"I don't know. I love that the birth went smoothly. I was worried there'd be complications. But now that it's all over, what's next?"

"What do you mean? We can just go home and—"

"I mean I'm worried about the world. What kind of climate will our daughter grow up in? Should we move out of Miami before the whole city goes underwater?" She shook her head and sighed. "Every time I look at those IPCC charts, I envision what the world will be like in each emission scenario. I imagine what ordinary people's lives will be like if we follow that path. It used to just be a thought experiment. But now..."

Kandace frowned. She felt tears welling up in her eyes, but tried not to cry. Instead, she squeezed Abe's hand and held her baby close.

Abe squeezed back, tears forming in his own eyes.

"I'm sure it'll be alright. They finally signed a climate agreement. We'll be on the low emissions track in no time. Little Ava will learn about the climate crisis in history class! 'Yes, children, we almost rendered our planet uninhabitable. But your parents got organized and brought us back from the brink!'"

Kandace laughed. "We should be so lucky. I'll be happy if she makes it to her eighteenth birthday without Miami going underwater."

Abe smiled.

"Me too."

They squeezed each other's hands and looked at Ava. Shortly after they stopped talking, Ava finished nursing and they all drifted off to sleep.

Emissions Scenario 1
Miami, Florida
December 12, 2065

Ava blew out the candles on her chocolate birthday cake. Everyone sitting around the dining room table clapped and cheered. As the smoke cleared, Ava pulled the waxy "5" and "0" out of the cake, setting them aside for reuse.

"Grandma! Grandma! What did you wish for?"

The adults all laughed, including Ava. Little Kandy was Ava's only grandchild. As much as Ava appreciated having her brother, nephew, niece, and three children at family gatherings, it was refreshing to have a small child in the family again. Kandy was four years old, and her youthful exuberance and intellectual curiosity always brought a smile to Ava's face.

"Birthday wishes are a secret, Kandy. If I say it out loud, it won't come true!"

"But why are they secret, Grandma?"

"That's a good question, Kandy. I don't know."

"I can keep a secret, Grandma! You can tell me! Please!"

Ava smiled. "Alright, Kandy. Just this once."

Kandy hopped out of her chair and ran to her grandmother's side. Ava cupped her hand and leaned in close to whisper in Kandy's ear.

"I wished for more happy birthdays with you!"

Kandy laughed. Ava pressed her finger against her lips, making a shushing noise. Kandy imitated her grandmother, nodding knowingly as she returned to her seat.

Ava's brother Noah cut the cake and passed slices around the table. After a few minutes of cake and conversation, Noah asked the question she knew he would ask eventually.

"Ava, are you sure you want to go to this debate? It's your birthday! Can't someone else go?"

Ava shook her head and smiled. "There's always something on my birthday, Noah. I was born on the original Fossil Free Day! It wouldn't be right for me to skip a Fossil Free celebration. I haven't missed one yet."

"Of course. But why a debate? Why don't you just relax and celebrate how far we've come in the past fifty years?"

"What an awful thing to say on Fossil Free Day! We never would've made it this far with that attitude. As long as there are still people in Tallahassee and Washington pushing fossil fuels, the struggle continues."

Noah sighed. "Alright, Ava. Good point. I just want you to be happy."

"I am happy. Now let's finish this cake and head to the debate."

———◉———

Ava and her family stepped off the electric tram and into the crowd streaming down 27th Avenue. The four traffic lanes and strip of forest garden in the median were overflowing with thousands of people. Most were on their way to the stadium or neighborhood Synergy Center, but Ava was excited to know that some of them were here to see her speak.

The street was large enough that it usually had significant electric vehicle traffic, but today most streets had been closed for the holiday. It was a boisterous crowd, with people laughing and talking excitedly as they walked to Fossil Free Day events throughout Miami.

After walking for a few minutes, Ava and her family reached the Miami-Dade County Auditorium. She led them to their seats, then said a quick goodbye.

As Ava turned to leave, Kandy grabbed her hand.

"I want to come with you!"

Ava smiled. "I know, Kandy. But Grandma will be busy on stage. Can you sit here with the rest of the family like a big girl?"

Kandy sighed, crossing her arms and pouting.

"Okay, Grandma. I guess so."

"Thanks, sweetie. I'll come and say goodbye when it's all over."

Ava kissed Kandy lightly on the forehead. Then she waved to the rest of her family and headed toward the stage.

———◉———

The auditorium was nearly filled to its capacity of over two thousand people. There were also thousands of online viewers. Ava's talks and debates usually drew tens of thousands of people, but so much was happening on Fossil Free Day that any one event could only draw so many attendees.

There were three people on stage: Ava, the moderator, and Lucretia Adelaide, spokesperson for the American Petroleum Institute. API wasn't the political and economic juggernaut that it had been when Ava was growing up, but it was still the largest trade association for what was left of the oil and gas industry. Ever since the campaign finance reforms of the '20s had stopped fossil fuel lobbyists from buying candidates, they had been forced to peddle their product directly to an increasingly hostile public. Calling them out on past crimes and present lies was a time-honored Fossil Free Day tradition.

When the moderator introduced Lucretia, the audience erupted into boos, hisses, and angry shouting. There were a few hundred people near the back who cheered, but they were drowned out by over a thousand detractors. The moderator asked the crowd to settle down so he could introduce the next speaker.

Ava was speaking in her role as executive director of the Miami Fossil Free Coalition. When the moderator announced her name, most of the audience burst into rowdy applause and cheering. The moderator called for quiet again so that the speakers could present their opening remarks.

Lucretia's remarks were short and impersonal. She emphasized the same talking points that API had used for several decades. Yes, human-caused global warming was a terrible crisis—but she claimed that the worst was over and fossil fuel use was much cleaner than it used to be. She concluded that it would be prudent to keep consumption at current levels by exploring new reserves to replace those that had been shut down or depleted.

A few of her points were punctuated by sporadic outbursts of booing, but the audience mostly didn't interrupt. When she was done, the moderator thanked her and yielded the floor to Ava.

"Thank you for inviting me to speak today. My opening remarks will be brief. They will consist entirely of a reminder of why we are gathered here today."

"Fossil Free Day is an international holiday that we celebrate every year on December 12. This date was chosen in honor of the Paris Agreement of 2015. The Paris Agreement was the first time that the world's governments agreed to the goal of reducing greenhouse gas emissions enough to keep global warming well below 2 degrees Celsius."

"As we now know, the promises made by governments weren't enough. Even after the Paris Agreement, we were still on a fast track to disaster. Therefore, the first few Fossil Free Days were celebrated with global uprisings. For years, the world was swept up in a chaotic struggle for the future of this planet. Over the course of several decades, we the people transitioned our communities and societies toward more just and sustainable ways of living."

"Today, we live in an unprecedented age of technological advancement and social cooperation. For the first time in history, the vast majority of humanity has access to food, shelter, clean air, clean water, and clean energy. Those who profited most from climate disruption were held accountable. During the decade we now call Decade Zero, we spent trillions of dollars on everything from clean energy to transportation to the great sea walls and pumps that now protect many of the world's coastal cities. And in the end, we transitioned away from fossil fuels. The latest numbers indicate that less than 4% of our energy now comes from fossil fuels."

Ava turned to address Lucretia directly.

"After all of this—after you nearly destroyed the world with your product and we had to organize a global revolution to stop you—you still want to go after the last reserves of fossil fuels that you never got around to burning? You promise that it'll be cleaner this time and that we shouldn't let such incredible reserves of concentrated energy go to waste. You ask for permission to fire up your drills and put us on a fast track to disaster again."

"My answer to you, Ms. Adelaide, is no. No, we won't go back to the fossil fuels era. Not on my watch, and not on Fossil Free Day."

The crowd burst into jubilant applause, rising to their feet and cheering. The few people in the audience who supported Lucretia sat in their seats and fumed, surrounded by everyone who was applauding for Ava.

Emissions Scenario 2
Miami, Florida
December 12, 2065

Ava blew out the candle on her birthday cupcake. Before the puff of smoke cleared, she plucked the candle out of the cupcake, unabashedly licking up every last speck of frosting.

"Thank you, Mercedes! This is the first time I've had chocolate since my last birthday. How did—"

"I know a guy from the Roads who has a stockpile of cocoa. He bought it wholesale back when it was only thirty dollars a pound!"

"How much did you pay for it?"

Mercedes smiled. "Oh, don't worry about that, Ava. It's your birthday!"

"You shouldn't have. Thank you."

After Ava finished her cupcake, she and Mercedes left the apartment. They walked along the floating plastic planks that served as sidewalks for much of the city and headed down the flooded street toward the nearest HoverBus stop.

When they reached the corner, Ava and Mercedes climbed a rusty ladder that led up to a plywood catwalk two stories above the street. The rickety planks were the only way to cross without swimming through floodwater. They creaked and rattled as the two women inched across to the other side.

When they climbed back down to street level, Mercedes glared down the block at the next ladder.

"You know, Miami would have been better off if the oil barons had just burned through all their reserves! At least then the city would be so flooded that we'd all use boats and the city would put in real crosswalks. They have steel stairs and plexiglass platforms in the Roads and Brickell. Why can't we have that? These ladders and planks are killing me."

Ava nodded, rubbing her shoulder as they walked down the block toward the next ladder. Mercedes made the same complaint every time they went downtown. Ava had given up trying to object.

"They haven't killed us yet. But maybe that's the long-term plan. Maybe everyone without a yacht will fall and drown eventually." She sighed, shaking her head at the thought. "Come on, it's just a few blocks."

After making two more crossings over aging ladders and wobbly boards, they reached the HoverBus stop.

The HoverBus was the city's solution to citywide transit on flooded streets. Water levels varied from zero to six feet depending on location, rainfall, and tides. Many residents and some emergency services used boats and rafts because the water was usually deep enough for them. But boats would often bottom out if they took a wrong turn at low tide. Commuters needed something that could handle both solid ground and high water.

Although HoverBus routes reached all of Miami, they always ran late and sometimes never came at all. Passengers had to go to the stop and hope that a HoverBus would come eventually.

Ava and Mercedes made small talk with other passengers until the HoverBus arrived. The boxy green hovercraft was full of people with Fossil Free signs and T-shirts. They made more stops along the way, always picking up more passengers than they dropped off. Ava sat on Mercedes' lap so that an elderly woman with a cane could sit down. The aisle was so full of people that Ava worried the whole hovercraft would sink.

When they reached the stop near the Torch of Friendship, everyone got off. Thousands of people were streaming toward the Torch and neighboring Bayfront Park for the Fossil Free Day rally and march. It was a sunny day—unseasonably warm even for Post-Change Miami, with only a few clouds in the sky.

Ava and Mercedes approached the Torch. Vandalism by climate justice activists in the '20s and '30s had forced the city to change the tip of the monument from a natural gas flame into a solar-powered LED display. Whenever she came here, Ava thought it was funny that they still called it a torch since the flame was gone.

When they stopped near the Torch, Mercedes nudged Ava.

"Why aren't you speaking this year? Did you finally get tired of giving speeches?"

Ava smirked. "That'll be the day. No, Julia's speaking for Fossil Free Coalition. Now that I'm working more hours, I can't volunteer as much, so she's taking over as director."

"Oh." Mercedes' smile faded. "But you'll still come to rallies, right?"

"Always. Especially today. I was born on the original Fossil Free Day! It's in my blood."

A woman with a megaphone started the program. She introduced herself and twelve other representatives of local organizations. Some, like the Miami Fossil Free Coalition, had an obvious connection to Fossil Free Day. Others engaged in social service and advocacy that were impacted by the permanent flooding of the city, the displacement of hundreds of thousands of Miamians, and the global depression that had brought poverty to even the wealthiest cities.

Ava noticed that the speeches were getting shorter every year. Everyone knew why they were here. Most had lost homes to flooding, hurricanes, or rioting. All had felt the tremendous difference that five or six degrees Fahrenheit could make on a hot summer day. A year's worth of pent-up frustration could finally be released on Fossil Free Day.

Belaboring the point would accomplish nothing. People weren't here for talk. They were here for action.

After the last person spoke, the moderator announced that it was time to start the march. Before she even finished her sentence, the crowd cheered and sprang into action.

Suddenly, there was a wild rush to take the flooded street. Wave after wave of people leapt into the murky water that flowed freely through the streets of Miami.

Since the Torch of Friendship was near the street, Ava and Mercedes were among the first wave. Some people were wading through the hip-deep flood water, but most were swimming. The waders and slower swimmers like Ava were thoroughly splashed and often knocked over by more enthusiastic swimmers.

Ava swam as quickly as she could through the chaos of the first block of the "march," but her bad back and shoulder limited her pace. Once she was clear of the worst splashing and jostling, she switched to the backstroke.

The advancing waves of faster swimmers would soon join other "swimarchers" and "kayaktivists" in clogging the streets of downtown Miami and shutting down various corporate and governmental offices for the day. But Ava's days on the front lines were over. Numerous arrests and injuries at the hands of riot police and security contractors had left her barely able to swim and likely to disappear permanently if she were arrested again.

Ava wanted more than anything to surge ahead with the other swimmers like she had just a few years ago. Instead, she did the backstroke for as long as she could, then stopped swimming. As she floated on her back through the floodwaters, the wake of the next generation of climate activists carried her forward.

Emissions Scenario 3
New Miami, South Florida
December 12, 2065

Ava picked up the ripe navel orange. She pushed her thumb into a spot near the stem, pulling back a ragged strip of peel to reveal the pulpy orange and white flesh. Puffs of citrus scent filled the air as she removed the peel piece by piece, careful not to spill any juice. Once the peel was completely removed, she put it in a bowl and pulled the orange apart, eating one segment at a time as the sun rose over the ocean.

This was her first time eating an orange since returning to Miami two years ago. Almost all of the original varieties in South Florida had been lost to citrus greening, irregular rainfall, saltwater intrusion, and the chaos of the Collapse. There were, however, a few citrus groves that had survived or been replanted with hardier GMO varieties since the truce with North Florida in 2057. Most of the harvest was exported, and the few boxes that stayed in South Florida were impossibly expensive. This particular orange, however, had been given to her by the Mayor in honor of her recent election as the new director of Synergy 4.

Ava stared out at the ocean, her eyes tracing the imaginary shoreline that had once defined the eastern edge of Miami. She was old enough to remember life before the Collapse: sandy beaches teeming with tourists, streets bustling with gas-guzzling cars, countless planes flying overhead, restaurants overflowing with every type of food imaginable. Her childhood memories of how it looked, smelled, sounded, and felt were still so clear.

The shoreline seemed surprisingly different without its beaches, even though there were no new buildings and most of the old ones were still standing in various states of disrepair. Before the Collapse, the building that now housed Synergy 4 had been a hotel. Most of the Synergy centers were housed in reclaimed hotels. Hotels and office buildings offered a convenient mix of high-density living space and room for most or all of the necessary Synergy functions: indoor gardening, sustainable water treatment, clean energy, classes, and other community services.

Ava had stayed in this hotel once as a child. The view from her office balcony near the top of Synergy 4 was familiar, but so much had changed since her childhood: sandy shores submerged, streets converted into canals, cars replaced by rowboats and motorboats carrying passengers through abandoned sections of the city.

Ava finished her orange and brought the peel inside. She looked back at the balcony and sighed. She would love to spend her birthday reminiscing and looking out on the ocean, but there was so much work to do.

———◉———

"Stop! Everyone just calm down and shut up!"

Ava knew that telling people to calm down was rarely effective. But she wanted to yell too, and that was the least offensive thing she could think of to yell.

Meetings of the Provisional City Commission of New Miami had briefly been open to the public in 2056. Unfortunately, a suicide bomber from North Florida had infiltrated the audience on Fossil Free Day in 2056, killing three and wounding eleven, including two Commissioners. Since then, the seven-member Commission had met in secret at secure locations in downtown Miami. Today's meeting was in a cramped conference room in the City Hall basement.

When Ava raised her voice, the shouting subsided. The Commissioners were a rowdy bunch, and Ava had quickly become known as the most cool-headed and reasonable voice on the Commission. Her shouting led several Commissioners to stop talking immediately. The rest eventually followed suit.

"Alright. Let's try this again. Emma, please give us a quick summary of the proposal. Then we can discuss it one last time—a civil discussion, like adults—and make our decision."

Commissioner Emma Garcia sighed, looking down at her notes.

"There's a lot of legalese, but the basic proposal is fairly simple. North Florida is reactivating their natural gas infrastructure. They want to use a stretch of pipeline on land ceded to South Florida by the Treaty of 2057. In return, they're offering to sell us gas at cost and provide any technical assistance we need for our infrastructure."

"Where are they getting this natural gas?" Commissioner Angel Ramirez studied his copy of the proposal. "I don't see any mention of that here."

Emma shrugged. "It doesn't say. Does that matter? Gas is gas. We're done with it. Didn't we learn anything from the Collapse? We don't want to go down that road again."

Commissioner Rufus White raised a hand to interrupt. "Let's not be hasty. We're in desperate need of more energy to rebuild this city. Natural gas is cleaner than coal and oil. If we can just-"

"No it isn't." Angel pointed and glared at Rufus. "Everyone peddling natural gas has been saying that for a hundred years. It's still not true. That's why I asked about the source. They all leak, but some leak more than others. And we have to be sure we're not funding the Texan separatists. I will leave this Commission right now if we agree to fund the Texan separatists."

The room fell silent. When a Commissioner threatened to leave the Commission, they weren't just threatening to resign. They were threatening to pull their district out of the fairly young Provisional City Commission.

Eventually, Ava broke the silence.

"Angel is partially right. We need to know where this gas is coming from. But it's not coming from Texas. My sources say it's from Illinois."

"Illinois?" Angel thought for a moment. "Second wave fracking, right? More regulated than first wave. Maybe it's cleaner."

"Not really." Ava sighed, paging through her notes. "They tried regulating, but fracking is fracking. It all leaks methane and poisons groundwater. Locals shut it down for a few decades during the Collapse. But someone started it up again this summer."

The room was quiet for a few moments while everyone considered this new information. As Rufus was about to speak, Emma interjected.

"What do you think, Ava? Do you support this proposal?"

Everyone turned to Ava. She was the newest member of the Commission, but her cool head and close involvement with the Synergy centers went a long way with the other Commissioners. The Synergy centers had led the first effort to resettle Miami after it was largely abandoned during the Collapse. They were home to less than a quarter of the city's residents, but their history and technical contributions to post-Collapse infrastructure gave them disproportionate sway on city politics.

Ava stared at her notes, gathering her thoughts.

"I'm going to have to say no on this one. We need energy, but we'll find another way. And we don't want to betray frontline communities in Illinois that are fighting this new round of fracking. I know Illinois may seem a world away, but I remember a time when we were all part of one big nation."

Rufus glared at Ava, his face flushed with anger.

"And what? You're going to unite us all under the banner of one nation by angering our neighbors to the north? If we don't take this offer, they may fight us for it. Do you remember what it was like the last time we went to war North Florida? No, of course you don't. Because you fled to Cuba!"

The room erupted into chaotic shouting. Ava tried to bring the meeting back to order, but this time raising her voice had no effect. She was confident that Emma and Angel were on her side, and that Rufus could only muster one or two more votes in favor of the proposal. The outcome of the meeting had probably already been determined. Even so, it was apparently going to take another hour or two of bickering before Rufus and his allies relented.

———————◉———————

Ava looked out across the ocean. Spending all day and night working without celebrating her birthday had left her even more introspective than usual. She looked out on the ocean and found herself lost in thought.

The contrast between New Miami and the Old Miami of her youth was sharpest at night. In the daytime, she could pretend that Miami was essentially unchanged. Roads had often flooded even when she was a child. Maybe this was just King Tide wreaking temporary havoc. Maybe the heavy damage to buildings was just hurricane damage that would be repaired soon. Maybe Miami was just having a rough year and would bounce back to its former glory any day now.

But at night, the darkness told another story.

Ava looked out at the city. Some people still saw it as an abandoned ruin. She herself had abandoned it for almost a decade, barely surviving refugee camps and war zones long enough to make her way home. Most who left didn't survive, and most survivors didn't return. Most of the buildings were dark, without even glowing corporate logos or security lights to illuminate their outlines. Major streets were sparsely lit by solar-powered buoys that guided the few boats were out after dark.

As she looked out on the dim lights dotting the battered coast and the dark churning of the barren ocean, she decided that New Miami was, in fact, a broken city. A broken city in a broken world. She was trying to fix it—but a part of her knew it would always be broken.

———————⬤———————

Paris, France
December 13, 2015

———————⬤———————

Kandace awoke with a start. The baby started crying, rousing Abe from his slumber. After calming the baby and letting her nurse, Kandace tapped Abe's shoulder.

"Abe! You won't believe the dream I just had. It was more like three dreams. I've never had such vivid dreams in my life."

Kandace started explaining her three dreams. At first, Abe just nodded with mild interest. Eventually, he grabbed a notebook and started taking notes. When Kandace finished, almost an hour had passed.

"That's... Kandace, that's amazing. I don't know what to say."

"I don't either. But I know it wasn't just a dream. It felt so real. I know this sounds crazy, but it felt like I was looking at that chart with different emissions scenarios and seeing three different versions of our baby's real future."

Abe thought about the dreams, glancing at his notes. Suddenly, his eyes lit up.

"Did one of them feel more real to you? Which one do you think is really going to happen?"

"I-"

Abe looked at Kandace expectantly. Kandace paused, thinking long and hard about the question. When she realized the answer, her heart started racing.

"I don't know."

Fill The Gap

Illinois Route 13 was quiet as usual for Zoe's morning commute into Carbondale. She saw a pair of headlights a few miles back in her rearview mirror, and another two pinpricks of light even farther away down the road in front of her. But mostly, she had the three lanes of westbound Route 13 all to herself.

This was one of her favorite parts of her morning routine, especially at this time of year. The road and sky were still dark enough that a seemingly limitless expanse of stars was still visible overhead. The first hints of dawn were starting to rise above the treeline behind her. The moon hung low above Crab Orchard Lake, its crisp silver moonlight reflected in the calm waters below.

While she was admiring the view, a deer leaped directly in front of her car.

Zoe slammed on the brake pedal. The deer had run into the road just a few yards ahead of her. She had quick reflexes, but there was no avoiding it.

Her front fender slammed into the deer at nearly full speed. Her airbags deployed, and her face slammed into the driver side airbag. The large brown and white body of the deer crushed the front end of the car, tumbled over the hood, and crashed through her windshield, lodging in the cracked glass between the two front airbags.

Zoe squeezed her eyes shut as the car skidded to a full stop on the shoulder of the road, banging lightly against the guardrail in the process of stopping.

For a few seconds, she sat motionless in her seat with her eyes still shut. When she opened them again, she was confronted by the dead eyes, lolling tongue, and pointy antlers of a mature buck just inches away from her face. She reflexively squeezed her eyes shut again, unbuckling her seatbelt and squirming out of the car with her eyes still closed. Once she was out in the open, she took a deep breath, opened her eyes again, and stared at her car, blinking in disbelief.

This was real. There was really a deer lodged in her windshield.

———◉———

"I'm sorry, ma'am. It looks like your claim was denied."

Zoe was sitting in an uncomfortable wooden chair in her insurance agent's small back office. The agent, a middle-aged white man named Ed Waterman, handed the denial letter back to her.

"But... I hit a deer! That isn't covered?"

"No, ma'am. That would be covered under comprehensive insurance, which is not included in your plan."

"So what do I do?"

The agent shrugged. "That's up to you, ma'am. The car's totaled, but you could sell it for scrap. Now that the Act's kicking in though, replacing it's going to be a problem."

"Act? What Act?"

"The Illinois Climate Mitigation and Adaptation Act. ICMA."

He pronounced the abbreviation as "ich-mah" like most people she'd heard talking about it. She'd read the term far more often than she'd heard it spoken, though, so it still sounded strange.

"Oh. Did that kick in already?"

"Yes ma'am. Start of the month."

"Oh. Okay. I thought it was end of the year for some reason."

"End of the fiscal year in June. I'm looking forward to next year's carbon tax rebate, personally. That's the best part of the bill. But a lot of folks around here are going to be hit hard by the used car ban."

"Used car ban?" Zoe's pulse quickened. "I thought they were only banning sales of new internal combustion engines."

"That happened in some states. Almost happened here too. But the Illinois legislature brought the ban hammer down hard. No new or used gas-guzzler sales. Period. You're the second client this month who's had their old junker totaled and couldn't get a new one. Of course, his claim was covered, so he'll at least get a scooter or one of those little smart cars out of the deal. He hasn't decided yet."

The agent looked around at several tidy stacks of papers on his semi-cluttered desk. After a few seconds, he found a stack of brochures and handed one to Zoe.

"This here's a list of new and used auto dealers in Southern Illinois. I wouldn't hold your breath for a cheap used electric around here, though. You may have to go up to St. Louis or even Chicago. Your best bet may be to save up for a scooter if that'll work for you."

Zoe sighed.

"Okay, thanks."

She stood up, tucking the brochure and the claim denial letter in her back pocket. The agent stood up with her and shook her hand.

"No problem. You have a good one, Ms. Hammond. Let me know if you have any other questions."

"I will. Thanks."

Zoe walked out of the office and left the building. As she walked down the street, she maintained her composure for the first few yards. But when she reached for her phone, her face flushed with anger, and she felt tears in her eyes. She slowed to a stop, taking a few deep breaths to calm herself.

Eventually, Zoe stepped off of the sidewalk and into the grass. She leaned against the trunk of a tree and sighed, pulling out her phone and calling a cab.

———◦———

The bicycle ride into Carbondale was an opportunity for Zoe to experience the scenic landscape of Southern Illinois even more intimately than she had during the morning commute in her old car. On some level, she enjoyed cycling through woodland, farmland, and quiet residential streets on the edge of town at dawn to reach her final destination on the Southern Illinois University campus. But that didn't quite make up for the difficulties of the switch from a gas-guzzling clunker to a rusty old bike. After a few harrowing close calls while riding on the shoulder of Route 13, she opted for a more hilly route on the back roads. More hills and more back roads meant getting up earlier and spending much more time and effort on her morning commute.

When she arrived on campus, the bike ride and the wet chill of the mid-October morning left her feeling an odd combination of cold and overheated. After locking up her bike at the nearest bike rack, she walked toward her first class. She was so lost in thought about her bike route and her homework that she almost walked right past the information table without noticing that someone was talking to her.

"Climate meeting tonight! Learn more about ICMA and other responses to climate change! Free pizza and vegan chili!"

Zoe paused, taking a few steps toward the small folding table full of brochures and flyers.

"ICMA?"

A young woman in a jeans jacket who looked like she was barely out of high school rose to her feet to greet Zoe.

"Yes! Illinois Climate Mitigation and Adaptation Act. Now that it's in effect, we're talking about all the benefits and next steps locally for climate action."

"Benefits." Zoe chuckled. "Do you want to hear about the problems, too?"

The smile faded from the young woman's face.

"I don't know. What problems?"

"Problems like people being stranded out in rural Williamson County because their old gas-guzzler got wrecked and they can't afford a new electric."

"Oh." The young woman paused, thinking it over. "I'm sure that's fine. Actually, we'd love to hear about it. There's been a lot of debate about how to handle that sort of thing." She handed Zoe a bright green quarter sheet flyer with details about the meeting. "It's tonight at 6pm."

"Sounds good. I'll be there." Zoe tucked the flyer into her back pocket. "And I hope you all have some good answers about 'that sort of thing.' It's not just a hypothetical."

She gave a polite wave to the young woman and the other people at the table, then headed off to class.

———◉———

The small meeting room was packed beyond its seating capacity. Thirty people sat around a central square composed of several plastic folding tables. Ten more people stood along one of the walls near the tables. Another wall was home to a two-table buffet with several boxes of pizza, two pots of chili, several boxes of canned sodas, and various potluck-style side dishes.

Alexis, the young woman Zoe had met earlier, was at the head of the table facilitating the meeting.

"Alright. I have a question based on what everyone said in their introductions. How many of you are here to complain about some aspect of the Illinois Climate Mitigation and Adaptation Act?"

Zoe raised her hand. She was surprised to see over half of the people around the room raise their hands too.

Alexis sighed. "And how many of you actually believe in global warming?"

Three people lowered their hands, but almost half of the room still had their hands raised.

"Okay. Well, we won't be debating the reality of global warming, so anyone who was planning on doing that is welcome to leave. Everyone else, let's talk details."

Alexis started calling on people around the table to describe their concerns about ICMA. The details varied, but they all came back to the same theme: cost of living. Prices for food, gas, and other necessities had already started going up due to the hefty carbon tax associated with ICMA. All Illinois taxpayers were going to receive an ICMA rebate that would in theory be greater than the cost of living increase. But that wouldn't come in until people received their tax refunds next year—and even then, it might not be enough for some people.

When it was Zoe's turn to talk, she leaned back in her chair and shrugged.

"I don't know. Don't get me wrong. ICMA's great in theory. I'm terrified about climate change. Half of Miami's underwater for good now, and a lot of cities and towns on the coasts aren't doing much better. And I have two uncles and a few cousins who farm around here, so I know these floods and droughts are killing Southern Illinois agriculture. We need to cut our emissions to zero as soon as possible. And all of these state-level bills that've been passing lately are already putting a major dent in our emissions. And they say ICMA's the best one since the one in California."

Zoe took a deep breath, pausing to gather her thoughts before continuing.

"But what about us? What about the people who can't wait a year for a tax rebate that may or may not be enough to pay the bills? What about people like me who get our old gas-guzzler totaled by a deer and can't replace it because we can't afford electric? What do we do?"

Most of the people in the room clapped. Alexis nodded, waiting for the room to quiet down before continuing.

"I agree 100%. When green groups were pushing for ICMA, we wanted all of the proceeds of the carbon tax to go to projects that combined aspects of clean energy transition and poverty alleviation. But in order to get the votes, most of that was cut in favor of tax rebates for businesses and a flat personal rebate for everyone in Illinois."

Zoe shook her head. "That doesn't seem right."

Alexis nodded again. "No, it doesn't. So the question now is what do we do about it? How can we meet people's needs in our local community while still doing everything we can to reduce our emissions?"

Zoe thought for a moment.

"Well, it seems to me we need to fill the gap. Fill the gap between now and that rebate next April. Fill the gap for poor folks who need transportation because of high gas prices and the gas-guzzler ban. Maybe we can get some grants, or do some fundraisers, or just pool our resources. Something to fill the gap for people left behind by ICMA."

"Fill the gap. I like that." Alexis wrote a note on her tablet computer. "Sounds like we may need to start a Fill the Gap committee. Anyone interested?"

Zoe raised her hand. As she looked around the room, another person slowly raised their hand. A third soon followed suit. Eventually, almost half of the people present raised their hands.

———————— ◉ ————————

Zoe was working on her final paper for one of her social work classes on her laptop when Alexis's head peeked out of her office doorway.

"Hey, I'm leaving town in a few hours. Can anybody else distribute the last round of off-campus flyers?"

There were eight volunteers in the lobby of the community center, including Zoe. All of them had their attention divided between eating leftover vegetarian stew from last night's Fill the Gap weekly potluck and typing intently on laptop keyboards or tablet screens. One was sitting at the front desk, two were at small side tables, and five were lounging around on mismatched sofas and armchairs that gave the lobby the look and feel of a retro living room.

When Alexis spoke, all but one of them glanced up from their glowing rectangles and started looking around to see if there were any other takers. After a few seconds, Zoe sighed and raised her hand.

"I've got it. I'm headed off campus anyway."

Alexis smiled. "Thank you! They should still be next to the printer. You're a lifesaver, Zoe."

Zoe spent another half hour working on her paper and replying to a few emails. Then she slid her laptop into her backpack, picked up the flyers from the printer table, and headed out into the night.

The streets and sidewalks of Carbondale were covered in a wintry mix of snow, ice, and freezing rain. It wasn't the worst weather she'd seen in town, but it was enough to keep her alert and tense as she biked around to several downtown businesses, the public library, and a few other nearby spots with bulletin boards.

While she was posting the flyer at a laundromat, she paused for a moment to warm up a bit and get a better look at what she was posting. The flyer featured colorful but fairly generic images of people enjoying a party with text about the big event coming up this weekend.

"FILL THE GAP Farm-To-Table Feast! Enjoy the finest local foods Southern Illinois has to offer while raising money for a good cause. Feast includes local wine, beer, and non-alcoholic cider. Live music, children's games, electric scooter raffle, and more. Proceeds benefit Fill The Gap, a new initiative offering weekly potlucks, utility bill help, transportation help, and other services to people adversely affected by ICMA. Come support climate justice, learn more about local climate-friendly food, and enjoy our harvest feast!"

Zoe nodded approvingly. The utility and transportation help were still mostly just ideas at this point due to lack of funding. But they had helped someone stop their power from being shut off, and the new carpooling club was growing in membership every week. With more funding, they could obviously do much more.

If the transportation assistance program raised enough money, she might even be able to get a vehicle sooner rather than later, which would be a pleasant change from her current daily commute in increasingly cold and wet weather.

When she finished reading her own flyer, she decided to skim the other flyers. Most were unremarkable, but when she noticed one of them, her eyes froze. It was a slick color flyer with a picture of a young male college student holding two giant bags emblazoned with glittery green dollar signs.

"Tired of waiting for your ICMA refund? FILL THE GAP! Get your ICMA Refund Loan at Payday Loans Unlimited! No credit check. Everyone's eligible! Offer ends December 31. ACT NOW!"

There were pull-tabs at the bottom of the flyer with a phone number and email address. Two of the dozen tabs had already been pulled.

Zoe felt her face flush in anger. Someone had taken their idea and turned it into a payday loan scam. It couldn't be a coincidence. The phrase "Fill The Gap" was too specific.

She found the thought of someone targeting people put out by ICMA infuriating. These payday loan places were notorious for taking advantage of low-income people during their hour of need. Offer a loan, charge the maximum legal amount of interest, and get people locked into a vicious cycle of needing a loan every payday.

And yet in spite of her anger, she found herself reaching for one of the tabs.

For a moment, she gripped one of the glossy paper tabs between her thumb and index finger. She wanted to let go, but her grip lingered. This was a one-time ICMA loan, not the usual payday loan scam. Were the interest rates really that bad? If she got one of these loans, would she be able to get a scooter or car right away? Before the worst of winter set in?

She let go of the tab, glaring at the slick image of the happy college student holding his ridiculously oversized bags of money. Before she had time to lose her resolve, she ripped the payday loan flyer off of the bulletin board, threw it in the trash, and stormed out the door.

The bike ride to her last few stops didn't feel cold and harrowing anymore. Something about the mix of posting good flyers and tearing down bad ones filled her veins with enough fire to keep her going through the biting wind and sleet. At every stop, she posted her flyers and threw the other ones in the trash.

When she completed her rounds, she went back to a few of the early stops to check for more of the payday loan flyers that she may have missed. After about an hour of pedalling back and forth around downtown Carbondale, she was finally ready for the long ride home out into the country.

———◦———

Zoe stepped into the crowded kitchen, offering to relieve one of the dishwashers. Almost a dozen people were busily packing up leftovers from the Fill The Gap Farm-To-Table Feast, bringing empty serving bowls and plates to the kitchen, and washing and drying dishes at the large stainless steel commercial sink. A middle-aged woman at one end of the sink handed Zoe a washcloth and let her take her place at the soapy scrubbing station.

After spending a half hour washing dishes, Zoe left the kitchen and went back to the community dining room to check messages on her phone and drink some more hard cider. While she was scrolling through her newsfeed, Alexis walked into the room and slumped down in a nearby chair, sighing heavily.

Zoe looked up from her phone and turned to Alexis.

"Tired?"

"Yes. But now that it's over, we'll all have a few days to recover."

"How'd we do?"

Alexis sighed again. "It was a wonderful event, and the turnout was good, but we didn't meet our goal. Not by a long shot. Hardly anyone donated beyond the door charge. We covered expenses and got enough to fund a little more food and utility aid, but not enough for the transportation assistance. I'm sorry, Zoe."

Zoe felt her stomach churn. Without transportation assistance, it would take her at least a few more months to save up enough money for even a small electric scooter. Maybe even longer. She'd definitely be spending the rest of the winter carless.

"It doesn't matter. Food and utilities are the important thing anyway. A lot of people will eat good meals and keep the lights on because of the work we did here today."

Alexis nodded. "That they will."

"And we'll keep pushing our other options for the transportation problem. It's not like it's just my problem. It's going to be a rough year or two for a lot of people around here who can't replace a broken-down car or keep up with rising food and gas prices. We need to work on that funding proposal for the city to help out first-time EV owners, and we need to get more volunteers from the university working on those grant proposals."

"Definitely." Alexis sat up in her chair, looking over at Zoe thoughtfully. "You know, I'm glad you're getting involved and sticking with it. You're starting to do more than me, and I've been at this for years."

Zoe laughed.

"I'm glad I got involved too."

———◈———

Zoe unlocked her bike from the metal rack outside of the community center and started the long bike ride home. The streets and bike lanes were fairly clear, but a slow, steady snowfall was starting to cover the city in a light dusting of wet off-white snow.

By the time Zoe made it out of town, the backroads were coated in a few inches of the sort of grey wintry slush that wasn't nearly as bad to ride on as ice, but still posed a hazard to reckless cyclists and drivers. She slowed her pace to what felt like a crawl, making sure that her headlight and taillight were both working so that if any cars did show up on the quiet road, they would see her.

The slow pace gave the cold and damp more time to seep through her several layers of protection from the elements. On the bright side, it also gave her more time to admire the sight of so many trees covered in a thick coat of clear ice. That was one of her favorite parts of winter—not a great time to be on the road, but a time when the trees occasionally looked like enormous crystal sculptures and the whole snow-dusted landscape looked like the cover of Christmas card.

Her thoughts were drifting between the beauty of the land and the details of her next round of volunteer work when she noticed unexpected movement just a few yards ahead of her on the edge of the road. She pulled her rear brake handle hard, sliding through the slush as she came to a stop.

It was a deer.

Zoe's heart pounded in her chest. This wasn't the first deer she'd seen since the accident, but it was definitely the first one she'd seen up close. It was only a few feet away. Her whole body tensed, and she froze in place, eyeing the deer warily.

The deer was a full-grown doe standing on the side of the road at the edge of Zoe's headlight beam. When their eyes met, Zoe found herself wondering what the doe was thinking. A long moment of silence passed between them, staring into each other's eyes. Eventually, the doe walked across the road and disappeared into the woods.

Zoe stared into the shadows at edge of the woods, stunned speechless. Her heart was still racing from the encounter. After a few moments, she suddenly burst out laughing. The tension in her body melted away, leaving a relaxing rush of newfound energy in its wake.

As Zoe climbed back onto her bike and continued her ride home, she felt a strange sense of relief.

This wasn't how she had expected to spend the winter—riding home on the backroads every night through the snow and rain on a cheap used bicycle. Hopefully she would get that new electric eventually. And hopefully she would get it sooner rather than later.

But even if she didn't, she would survive.

Either way, she was actually starting to feel relieved that her old gas-guzzler was gone. One less internal combustion engine on the road meant fewer emissions, which would save lives in the long run. She was still frustrated that the transition was leaving her and a lot of other people behind. But as she biked through the snow and ice the rest of the way home, each pump of the pedals felt like a step in the right direction.

Welcome to Synergy Central

Genevieve sat down in one of the empty padded chairs on her side of the conference table. The nine people on the other side of the long wooden table were all wearing formal business attire: mostly button-down shirts and ties, although there was also a man in a green polo shirt and a woman in a blue blouse. Genevieve was wearing a flowing rainbow-colored blouse and black slacks—an easy compromise between her usual loud wardrobe and the expected dress code of an official city commission meeting.

"Please state your name and title for the record."

"Genevieve Clementine. I'm the director of Synergy Central over in Forest Park East."

"Thank you, Ms. Clementine. My name is Edgar Nicholson. I'm the chair of the Community Development Administration's new Climate Adaptation Grant Committee. You're here to speak on behalf of your organization's grant application, correct?"

"Yes, sir."

"Good."

Mr. Nicholson looked down at his tablet computer, reviewing his notes before continuing.

"Ms. Clementine, we've all reviewed your application at length. There's no need to go over all of the details, but we do have two questions. One is a question that we've been asking all of the applicants. The other is unique to your particular proposal. Are you ready to answer these questions?"

Genevieve smiled.

"I'll do my best, Mr. Nicholson."

"Good. Here's your first question, then. Can you tell us, very briefly, what sets your proposal apart? We received thirty-seven applications. What can you do for your neighborhood and the city of St. Louis that nobody else can?"

"Okay. That's an easy one."

Genevieve set her binder full of notes down on the table.

"I'm sure you've received a lot of impressive proposals. Photovoltaic installations. Energy efficiency retrofits. Electric vehicles. Rooftop gardens. Neighborhood composting. That sort of thing. Am I right?"

Most of the members of the committee nodded, including Mr. Nicholson.

"Now, these all meet the grant's stated goals of incorporating a climate adaptation element and a low-income community development element. But what's different about Synergy Central is that we can implement all of those projects, and then some."

One of the committee members—a middle-aged man with greying hair and a bright red tie—raised his hand and spoke.

"That's a bold claim, Ms. Clementine. Care to elaborate?"

"Certainly." Genevieve opened her binder and reviewed her notes. "Synergy Central has only been in operation for a little over a year. However, in that short period of time, we've already organized or co-sponsored eleven projects with climate adaptation themes. We see ourselves as a think tank and resource center where many such projects are conceived and implemented. Our emphasis is on projects that are either self-funding or actually generate income, like the community garden and the solar installation training program. We're able to get so much done because we have four part-time staff, a solid team of about forty volunteers, and a cluster of apartment buildings that we've converted into a large community center. This grant would allow us to expand into the vacant hotel next door and seed a whole new round of projects that we can't accommodate currently due to space or funding considerations."

Mr. Nicholson nodded. "Yes, we've been reviewing your current operations. Most of us are very impressed."

"Thank you, Mr. Nicholson."

A sly smile spread across Mr. Nicholson's face. "Don't thank me yet, Ms. Clementine. Your impressive record means that we have much higher expectations for what you're going to do with this grant money. Which leads me to our second question."

Mr. Nicholson paused, tapping and swiping his tablet for a few moments in silence. Eventually, he looked back up at Genevieve.

"This is a bit unusual, Ms. Clementine, but we have a request for a major amendment to your proposal. The City of St. Louis is looking for ways to provide emergency housing and other services to approximately four thousand climate refugees from the Gulf Coast and Eastern Seaboard. I assume you're familiar with the situation? Coastal residents displaced by recent flooding and the acceleration of sea level rise?"

Genevieve shifted uncomfortably in her seat.

"Yes, sir. I've been following the news. And I... my sister and brother-in-law were displaced by Hurricane Florence. That's part of what inspired my interest in getting Synergy Central off the ground here in St. Louis. Just because we're not on the coast doesn't mean we can't do something."

Mr. Nicholson nodded. "Yes. Well, our request is that you amend your proposal to include some way of providing food and long-term housing for at least fifty of these climate refugees."

Genevieve's eyes widened.

"I... give me a moment, please."

She paged through her binder, reviewing her grant proposal and other notes. While she was pouring over the details, Mr. Nicholson continued.

"This other building you're expanding into. It's an old hotel, correct?"

"Yes."

"With more than enough units to house fifty refugees?"

"Yes. But we had plans for..." Genevieve sighed, setting aside her notes. "We can do it."

"You can, Ms. Clementine?" A look of relief flashed across his face. "You're sure?"

"Yes, I'm sure. I'll need some time to work out the details, of course. But I already have a few ideas. We wanted to house and feed about twenty eventually anyway. This just expands the need and accelerates the timeline."

"Yes. Well, we can't formally approve your proposal until we review your amendments. We'll need those amendments within the next thirty days. But coming up with a serious plan for these refugees will guarantee the success of your proposal."

Genevieve breathed a sigh of relief. "Thank you, Mr. Nicholson."

"Thank you, Ms. Clementine."

———————◉———————

"We can't do it!"

Quinn Nash stood up and stepped away from the table in the Synergy Central staff meeting room, closing his eyes and running his hands through his short black hair with a frustrated sigh. His face was normally very pale, but it flushed lightly whenever he was excited or angry.

Genevieve leaned back in her chair and shook her head with a smile. The other two people at the table leaned forward slightly, eyes glued to the latest round of fireworks between Quinn and Genevieve.

"Oh ye of little faith, Quinn. Look at what we've already accomplished! We've turned these old apartments into a fully functional green residence and community center in under a year. Permaculture garden, greywater systems, solar panels, solar hot water, tool library, green job training, the works. Half of our volunteers said it couldn't be done, not to mention what some of the haters had to say about us. But we did it. Here we are."

Quinn shot Genevieve an exasperated look. "That was different, Gen. We hit the ground running with some hefty donations and about two dozen volunteers with plenty of time on their hands. Now we're all overextended just keeping this place up and running."

Quinn sat back down and looked across the table at Genevieve. "Look, I get it. You want this grant. I do too. We need it to do the expansion—and the expansion's going to be amazing. But it was already pushing us all to our limits. And now this?" He waved a hand dismissively at Genevieve's stapled packet with the amendments to the grant proposal. "We'll have less than half the space we planned on for community projects. And we'll have thirty more people to house and feed than we planned. And we'll have them all here a year earlier than we planned. It shifts us from being a synergy center to a refugee camp—which is fine, on some level. But those refugees are taking up space that was meant for some of our most ambitious green design projects. The whole project's simply not going to be economically sustainable with more mouths to feed and fewer green projects to generate revenue."

Genevieve leaned forward, her smile fading from her lips. "I know it won't be easy, Quinn. You and the rest of the design team put together some amazing plans for the new building. But you know what? We can still do most of those new projects if we put our minds to it. We just have to get creative in our use of shared space. And I guarantee you that these fifty people who are about to walk through our doors will be a resource, not a liability. Don't think of this as fifty new bodies to house and mouths to feed. Think of this as fifty new volunteers who happen to need a place to stay."

Quinn sighed. "I hope you're right. When you put it that way, it does sound a little more encouraging."

Genevieve smiled. "I do what I can. Does that mean I can go ahead and turn in these amendments?"

Everyone around the table, including Quinn, nodded in agreement. Genevieve picked up her copy of the amendments and rose to her feet.

"Alright, then. I'll send them in right away. Here's hoping that we have the pleasure of meeting those fifty smiling faces sometime soon."

———●———

A long white bus pulled into the parking lot of Synergy Central's newly acquired vacant hotel. The bus almost looked like an old gas-powered school bus, but it was more boxy and had sealed storage compartments on the bottom like a passenger bus. Genevieve wondered if it was a repurposed prison bus or if it had always been used for disaster response and refugee transport.

As people started stepping off the bus, Genevieve, Quinn, and several other volunteers greeted each of them personally, welcoming them to Synergy Central and offering to help carry any luggage or other personal effects. The bus door was only a few yards away from the entrance to the lobby, so most people didn't need any help. But many seemed to appreciate the gesture.

The incoming residents were an interesting mix. Almost half of the fifty-three people who stepped off the bus had no luggage whatsoever. They looked visibly disheveled—some with stained or mismatched clothing, others with simple grey and white clothing that may have been issued by a charity or relief agency. The other half all looked like they had packed for a long trip away from home—suitcases, backpacks, purses, carry-on bags, laundry bags, pillows, blankets, even a few briefcases and old laptop bags. At a glance, there were more women than men, and a disproportionate number of Latinos, some speaking to each other in Spanish or in English with a strong accent. Genevieve wondered if they were part of another wave of refugees from Miami or elsewhere in South Florida.

After spending a few minutes greeting the new arrivals, Genevieve headed inside to see how the registration process was going.

Synergy Central volunteers were using the hotel's old lobby as a welcome center for the new arrivals. The people at the front desk gave incoming residents their initial room assignments and information packets about Synergy Central and the newly expanded housing program. There were also two folding tables next to the check-in station with several social work interns talking to the newcomers about how they were coping with their displacement and what help, if any, they may need from other local agencies.

Genevieve had scheduled an hour between the bus arrival and the orientation so that people would have time to find their new rooms and settle in a bit beforehand. That hour flew by quickly for her as she floated around helping new people to their rooms and helping volunteers troubleshoot a few minor glitches in the intake process. Before she knew it, she was standing in a stuffy hotel ballroom in front of a room full of people waiting to start their official orientation.

"Good afternoon! My name is Genevieve Clementine and I'm the director of Synergy Central. We're a community center where people work together on many different projects with an environmental justice and climate justice focus. Our emphasis is on projects that are either self-funding or actually generate income, like community gardens and green job training. We use the term synergy because we believe that having all of these projects together in one place creates a lot of benefits. They can share resources, brainstorm solutions together, build momentum for each other, and so on."

Genevieve scanned the crowd as she spoke. The new residents were sitting in several rows of thinly-padded stackable chairs that were all facing her small podium at the front of the room. Some were listening intently while others were idly paging through the information packets or just relaxing in their seats without paying much attention. Most were somewhere in between.

"Up until a few days ago, we were operating out of the apartments next door. Now, we're expanding into this vacant hotel—and we want you to be a part of this expansion. As a part of your agreement with Synergy Central, you'll be asked to contribute a minimum of twenty hours per week of volunteering. Anything you do for any one of our active projects will count toward this total. In return, you'll receive a place to stay, three meals a day, and a voice on our governing council, just like every other resident and volunteer."

A middle-aged man in the audience raised his hand.

"Twenty hours? That's it? That's a better deal than I had before the hurricane."

There were a few laughs in the audience. Genevieve smiled and nodded.

"Yes, that's it. We'll have you fill out a skills inventory to help you figure out which of our projects will be a good fit for you. And if you're unable to volunteer for any reason, we'll give you a waiver. We need a lot of help right now, but we don't want to penalize you if you have health difficulties or other challenges that prevent you from volunteering. Any other questions?"

She looked around the room. No one else raised their hand.

"If there are no other questions, I'll turn it over to our program coordinator, Quinn Nash. He'll be filling you in on some of the logistical details of your stay here at Synergy Central and the other programs you can volunteer for or take advantage of. Thank you again—and welcome to Synergy Central!"

———◦———

The parking lot and rooftop of the old hotel were filled with people working in the hot midday sun. Some were moving soil, tools, and other gardening supplies to the new garden plots in the parking lot and on the roof. Others were installing solar panels, a solar hot water system, and a greywater system on the roof and sides of the building. A teenager in overalls and a loose-fitting T-shirt was painting over the boxy sign next to the parking lot entrance. The freshly painted sign said "SYNERGY CENTRAL," in big, bold letters, with the building's new name, "Pueblo Nuevo," painted below it in smaller print.

Genevieve took a break from building compost bins and walked around to the various workstations to see how everything was progressing. It was the biggest work day they'd had since the new residents had arrived on the bus a few weeks ago. So far, everything seemed to be going well. The addition of more electricity, water, and food would go a long way to make the new residents more comfortable and support the non-residential projects they had planned in other parts of the building.

After talking to a few people in the parking lot, she headed up four flights of stairs to the roof.

What was once an empty expanse of black tar with a couple of air conditioning units peeking through it was rapidly transforming into a multi-purpose green roof. Workers from a solar energy company were installing steel racks that would soon hold numerous rows of traditional photovoltaic panels. The racks had been specially designed to leave space underneath to grow mushrooms and plant varieties that prefer shade. The rest of the roof was devoted mostly to garden plots and narrow walking paths, with wider accessible paths in an area devoted to raised bed gardening.

There was still plenty of work to be done, but it looked like most of the groundwork had been laid in a single intensive afternoon of labor provided by a mix of paid solar installation staff, Synergy Central volunteers, and other assorted volunteers from the local community.

Genevieve paused for a moment just to take it all in. She walked up to a railing and looked out over the parking lot and the neighboring apartment buildings that also belonged to Synergy. While she was admiring the view, she heard footsteps and a voice from just over her shoulder.

"Not bad for a bunch of misfits and refugees, eh Gen?"

Genevieve turned around and smiled when she saw Amalia Abaroa, the woman that new and old Synergists alike had taken to calling Abuelita. She was a short, lean woman with long grey hair, lively brown eyes, and dark tan skin, though not as dark as Genevieve's own complexion. Her flowing green blouse looked elegant and comfortable, and her worn jeans and boots looked eminently practical for a day of gardening.

"Abuelita. So good to see you. How's everything been over here at Pueblo?"

"Oh, I can't complain. My old house is underwater, so anything's an improvement."

Both women smiled. Genevieve looked around at some of the other new residents who were hard at work transforming the dream of a green roof into a reality.

"How is everyone settling in? They seem to be putting in a lot of good work today. Are people adjusting?"

"Oh, yes, mostly." Abuelita followed Genevieve's gaze, nodding approvingly. "Everyone is very grateful. Some people are already talking about making Pueblo Nuevo their permanent home."

"But?"

"But..." Abuelita sighed. "There's no taming the youth, you know? I'm content here so far. I may live out the rest of my days here, if the days keep going well. I like to garden and help in other ways. But the youth... they want something more than food and shelter. They want."

"I see. And what about the green jobs program? Are any of them interested in the solar training or energy efficiency training?"

"Oh, they like it. Some of them like it, anyway. But there's anxiety, you know? There are a lot of people right now washing up on these inland shores, looking for jobs. And there are good green jobs out there, but are there enough? We have food and shelter, but what they want is a future. They want to save money, buy a house, have a safe place for their kids, or for retirement." She paused, choosing her words carefully. "They want Synergy Central to spend all of its time and energy on green jobs instead of dabbling in a dozen other green projects."

"I see." Genevieve looked off into the distance, lost in thought. "We do have an emphasis on projects with economic benefits. But we also seek diversity of projects so that we can serve as a regional model for the Greater St. Louis area."

"Yes. This is very good for the city. But it will be an issue with residents who want to focus on green jobs. And Pueblo residents are now a narrow majority on the Synergy Central council, yes?"

"Yes."

"You see, then, what might happen." Abuelita sighed. "I actually tend to agree with you. I will talk to people about the value of these little green projects that Quinn and the others have been telling us about. They are good, and they might even create some jobs eventually. But at the next meeting, you may want to say something about some specific new project that will bring in more definite jobs. Even a few new job opportunities will ease everyone's minds."

Genevieve nodded. "I'll see what I can do. I've still got a stack of skills inventories and suggestions to review, so maybe I'll find something there. Thank you, Abuelita."

※

Genevieve, Quinn, and several other staff and volunteers sat around a table in the staff meeting room. Stacks of index cards and sheets of paper were scattered haphazardly across the table, mixed with several empty or half-empty reusable bowls, plates, and cups.

"I'm not seeing it, Gen." Quinn sighed, running his fingers through his hair. "I see some great leads here for traditional employment. Some of these folks have IT skills, managerial experience, hospitality, aviation, other things that look great on a resume. But the local labor market's flooded with refugees. We aren't going to find these people quality employment easily unless we help them create it. Entrepreneurship, maybe? Start your own business? But that involves a lot of risk and startup capital. No magic bullet there."

Genevieve shook her head. Her eyes shifted from the sheets of paper to the index cards.

"What about the project suggestion box?"

One of the volunteers picked up a stack of the hand-written suggestion cards and started thumbing through them.

"Not as much as we hoped. Most of the ideas are either too pie-in-the-sky or too similar to projects we're already doing."

"Pie in the sky. Why does that... wait a minute. That reminds me of something" Genevieve raised a hand to hold off any interruptions. "I've got an idea forming."

The room fell silent. Genevieve started rummaging through the stacks of paper and suggestion cards. After a few moments of searching, she came up with a single suggestion card and several skill inventory sheets.

"It's a long shot. But if it works, it'll be golden."

She handed the documents to Quinn. As he looked them over, the other staff and volunteers gathered behind him to read over his shoulder.

"I love it. I absolutely love it. But is it really possible? I can only imagine the startup capital involved..."

"Oh ye of little faith, Quinn." She leaned back in her chair, a broad smile spreading across her lips. "There are a lot of businesses and commuters in Greater St. Louis who need something like this. Gas prices are skyrocketing, and most individuals and businesses haven't transitioned to electric vehicles yet. We need a new transportation solution. This could be it."

"Alright. You've got my vote." He looked around the room. "What do you think? Let's see a show of hands. Should we give this a try?"

Everyone in the room raised their hand. Genevieve looked around the room and nodded approvingly.

"Good. I'll start working on the proposal for the next council meeting."

———◦———

Genevieve walked down a sidewalk that led into the park across the street from Synergy Central. The park was only a block long and wide, so it didn't take her long to reach the temporary stage that had been set up on one end of the multipurpose field that took up the majority of the park's open green space.

The ten foot by thirty foot platform was home to a simple wooden podium, microphone, and small black box speakers. About two dozen people stood on the platform—a mix of Synergists, city officials, and business representatives, all dressed in formal suits and ties or button-up shirts. Genevieve was wearing the same flowing rainbow-colored blouse and black slacks that she wore to most official functions. The audience standing in front of the platform was filled with about a dozen reporters and dozens of Synergists and local community members.

Genevieve started heading for the stage, then noticed Abuelita near the front of the audience.

"Abuelita! So glad you could make it."

"Yes, I wouldn't miss it." She leaned in closer, lowering her voice nearly to a whisper. "You already have a dozen people working for this project? With more to come? You really did it!"

"I didn't do this. We did it. Together." Genevieve looked around at the familiar faces in the audience and on the stage. "This wouldn't have been possible without the work of dozens of volunteers and several investors over the past nine months. What started as an idea on a comment card quickly evolved into..."

Genevieve's voice trailed off as she noticed something up in the sky. "There it is!"

A large aircraft was drifting into view from the west, peeking over the rooftops of Synergy Central in its final descent into the park. It looked like a blimp, but the balloon envelope was stretched into a flattened cigar shape by several rigid ribs. Four helicopter rotors protruded from the sides of the bottom half of the balloon. A large kelly green gondola was attached to the bottom, and a lightweight black cargo container dangled from the bottom of each of the rotors. The top half was covered in shiny photovoltaic solar panels, while the bottom half was a smooth surface that matched the kelly green of the gondola.

When people in the park saw the unusual aircraft, they burst into applause. As the dirigible approached, it soon became obvious that it would barely fit into the park. The gondola was easily small enough to fit into the multipurpose field, and the four cargo containers would fit with some room to spare. But the enormous green envelope that held the craft aloft was about as long as the entire park.

The dirigible turned slowly as it approached, aligning itself diagonally above the center of the multipurpose field. Soon, it drifted to a halt a few yards above the field, maneuvering the gondola over a large X on the ground before descending to a gentle landing on the grass.

The rotors slowed to a stop. Most of the people on and near the stage were now standing underneath the envelope of the dirigible. A hush fell over the crowd as several people in green flight suits emerged from the gondola and started tethering the dirigible to the ground.

Genevieve peeled her gaze away from the craft and looked over to the stage.

"That's my cue."

She strode over to the stage and approached the podium. After checking to make sure that the microphone was on, she spoke to the assembled crowd.

"Welcome to Synergy Central! And welcome to the inaugural flight of the next step in St. Louis' transition to cleaner and more affordable transportation system."

The crew of the dirigible walked over to one of the cargo containers and opened the doors. A forklift left the Synergy Central parking lot and approached the container.

"Dirigibles are one of several excellent solutions for commuter and industrial transportation. They require little or no infrastructure on the ground—just a field to land in or a structure to tether to. They produce fewer emissions and require little energy to operate since most of the heavy lifting is done by the helium that keeps them aloft. They can be easily modified to carry passengers, cargo, or both. Some people still see them as a relic or a novelty—but as materials costs have gone down and fuel costs have gone up, they've really started making a comeback, with new systems already popping up in New York City and a few remote industrial communities in the Arctic Circle. And now, the time has come for them to revolutionize the transportation sector of St. Louis!"

The crowd burst into a long and eager wave of applause. She had a few more remarks planned about how the project fit with the rest of Synergy Central's work—but the longer she looked up at the shiny green envelope of the dirigible floating overhead, the more she wanted to get a closer look. After saying a few words of introduction for the next speaker, she stepped down from the podium and approached the gondola.

———⚫———

Genevieve had never seen Synergy Central from above, except in old satellite photos that didn't reflect any of the improvements they'd made during their time operating out of the former apartment buildings and now the former hotel next door. As the dirigible rose high into the air, she caught a glimpse of what they'd all been working to accomplish over the past couple of years.

There were several rooftops full of rows of solar panels, rows and spirals of colorful flowers and garden greenery, black pipes and reservoirs for solar hot water and rainwater catchment, and the occasional glimpses of community sculptures and murals. She knew that there were also things that she couldn't see from above—green job training programs, community classes, movie showings, plays, brainstorming sessions, and other activities that were changing everything from the ways people look at the world to the ways they live in it.

As she looked out the gondola window, she heard a voice behind her.

"You know that this is going to take a lot more work."

Quinn stepped forward and joined her at the gondola window. They looked out at the scenery in silence for a while before he continued.

"We're not out of the woods yet. We're lucky we found an angel investor who was already working on commercial dirigibles. The road ahead won't be as easy. If we're going to sustain this project financially, we need at least a dozen more stops. We need a lot more paying customers, and we need to convince a lot of businesses to use a new type of transport."

"Road? I don't think we can call it a road ahead anymore now that we're flying."

Quinn laughed. "Good point."

"Seriously, though. Yes, I know it's going to be a lot of work—and we might not be able to make this particular project last. But you know what?"

"What?"

"I like the work." Genevieve smiled. "And I like the fact that the path ahead is long and full of surprises. I wouldn't have it any other way."

Spread The Sunshine

Torrential rain descended on downtown Miami with increasing intensity. Rivers of water flooded through city streets littered with abandoned cars and floating debris. Most of Miami's inhabitants had long since fled the city or hunkered down on higher ground, but some of those who had stayed behind to protect their homes and businesses were now rethinking that decision, pouring into the streets and fighting against the rising tide to find refuge somewhere above water.

Amalia Marisol stepped out of her flooded office building and into the deluge. The water was already up to her knees, making it difficult to walk against the current. But the only way to reach higher ground was to go uphill. She cursed herself for her rash decision to stay behind in an office building that she knew would almost certainly be flooded, but she was glad that she had the foresight to bring her bugout bag with her. The hefty camping backpack was full of food, tools, and a few important documents that would come in handy if she couldn't make it back to her apartment before leaving the city.

When Amalia reached the corner, she saw a cluster of five people half a block away walking in the opposite direction. She struggled to quicken her pace, calling out to them through the roar of wind and rain.

"Hey!"

The group didn't seem to hear her, but they were moving slowly enough that she knew she could catch up quickly. One of them was limping and being helped along by someone. The others were moving slowly to keep pace.

Once Amalia was within a few yards of the group, she tried shouting again.

"Hey!"

A middle-aged woman in a suit near the back of the group turned and motioned for Amalia to approach. Once she was within arm's length, she matched their pace and spoke again.

"Where are you going?"

The woman pointed down the street. "There's one last round of buses leaving the city a few blocks over. Jim has a sprained ankle, but we can get there in time if we hustle."

"Where are the buses going?"

"No idea. Any port in a storm though, right?"

"I guess so."

She walked over to the older man, also in a suit, who was limping and slid an arm under his shoulder. Now that there were two people helping him make his way down the street, the whole group moved a little more quickly.

"Alright, let's go."

———————◉———————

The rusty white bus pulled into a small but well-lit parking lot somewhere in New Orleans. The internal combustion engine at the front of the aging vehicle roared and rumbled one last time as the bus lurched across the cracked concrete to the far corner of the lot and rolled to a stop. Once the bus was parked, the engine sputtered into silence, and the folding door at the front hissed and clattered open.

Amalia stretched in her seat and looked out the window, half-expecting to see another gas station or rest stop. Instead, she saw a handful of small houses and a long red brick building with a worn grey roof that looked like it used to be a large grocery store. The words "Algiers Climate Justice Center" were painted directly on the roof in simple block lettering.

The bus driver stood up and stepped into the aisle, clearing her throat and clapping her hands together to get everyone's attention.

"End of the line, folks. Dispatch says this place is our best option. They've got cots and food and some case managers to help you figure out your next steps. I've been here before, they're good people. Just head on in the front door and they'll get you taken care of. Good luck, everyone."

Amalia shoved the folded shirt that she'd been using as a pillow back into her backpack and stepped into the aisle, slowly making her way off of the bus and into the parking lot along with the rest of the passengers.

When she stepped into the Algiers Climate Justice Center, Amalia was convinced that it had in fact been a grocery store or some other retail business in a previous life. Most of the interior consisted of a large open space with high ceilings that was subdivided into several smaller sections by a mismatched mix of desks, tables, gray metal shelves, and padded brown movable walls. Several people were moving the walls and tables in one corner of the building out of the way to make room for more cots and ground pads. She thought about stepping out of line and helping, but everything past the first four desks near the front entrance was blocked off by rope barriers.

Two volunteers were walking up and down the line of new arrivals offering water and snacks. Amalia chugged the water and devoured a small bag of pretzels. She had other food in her backpack, but she hadn't touched it yet since she wanted to make it last as long as possible while she was on the road.

After a few minutes of waiting, Amalia reached the front of the line and took a seat at one of the desks. A young woman in a T-shirt and jeans greeted her with a smile.

"Welcome to New Orleans! My name is Audrey. I'm here to help you get settled in for the night. Mind if I ask you a couple of quick questions?"

"Sure."

"Good." Audrey picked up a tablet computer and started entering. "What's your name?"

"Amalia. Amalia Marisol."

"Thank you, Amalia. Do you have any medical conditions you may need help with overnight? Allergies, sleep apnea, anything else that might cause you problems while you're sleeping?"

Amalia shook her head. "No, I'm healthy. It's been a rough day, but I'll be fine when I get some sleep."

"Well, hopefully you'll get some good sleep now that you're here." She tapped on her tablet and looked back up at Amalia. "Okay, next question. Are you trying to get to friends and family in another city? Or do you want help figuring out where to go from here?"

"Oh." Amalia paused. "Well, I don't really have any family who can take me in. And most of my friends just got flooded out of Miami too. So I guess I want help figuring out where to go."

"Okay, that's fine." Audrey tapped and swiped on the tablet. "We'll set you up with someone in the morning. Do you have any questions for me, or should we get you set up with a cot and blanket?"

"A cot sounds wonderful right now."

"Good! Patty here will get you set up. If you have any—"

Amalia raised her hand to interrupt.

"Actually, I thought of a question."

"Okay. What is it?"

"Do you have any job openings? I was a grant writer at a nonprofit back in Miami. I could do grant writing or maybe some program and fundraising work. I even have my"

Audrey looked up at Amalia, shaking her head with a sad smile.

"I'm sorry, hon, but I really doubt it. We don't really have funding for any new staff right now. I'm not even getting paid for tonight, honestly. We've got a few staff and a lot of volunteers filling in the gaps."

Amalia nodded. "Oh, that's alright. I know how it goes. It'll be a self-funding grant writing position though. Can I at least send you my resume?"

"Sure. I'll give you our director's email address."

Audrey fished through the desk drawers for a minute, then handed Amalia a business card.

"Here you go."

"Thank you."

"Anything else?"

"No, that's great."

"Good. I hope you enjoy your stay at the Climate Justice Center. And good luck with the resume!"

———◦———

Once Amalia and the other new arrivals were settled in, the Algiers Climate Justice Center was dark and quiet for the rest of the night. In spite of her exhaustion, Amalia found herself lying awake for what seemed like an hour or more, listening to the sounds of whirring air conditioning, creaking cots, and someone in another corner of the building with a hacking cough that came and went periodically. Eventually, she drifted off to sleep.

When she woke in the morning, half of the cots around her were already empty. A large white sign at one end of the sleeping area said "FOOD" in bold black letters, with an arrow pointing down an aisle of movable walls toward the far end of the building. Amalia folded her blanket, tucked her bulky backpack under her cot, and left in search of breakfast.

The dining area was relatively small and tightly-spaced, with eight plastic folding tables, several dozen metal folding chairs, and four food carts filled with a few trays of scrambled eggs and miscellaneous other cold foods: bagels, bread, apples, bags of chips and pretzels. What caught Amalia's eye even more than the food or people, though, was a small table with several power strips and charging cables for cell phones and tablets. She plugged in her phone, then helped herself to some eggs and apples.

Most of the morning was uneventful. She finished her breakfast, helped with the dishes, picked up her fully-charged phone, spoke to another case worker, and sent her resume to the director. As lunch came and went, and she found herself feeling increasingly restless. Eventually, she decided to go for a walk to explore the neighborhood she now found herself in. On her way out of the building, though, she heard someone calling her name.

"Amalia!"

Amalia turned to see a middle-aged woman in a green blouse and black slacks walking toward her.

"You're Amalia, right? I'm Kendra Williams, Director of the Algiers Climate Justice Center." She shook Amalia's hand. "I hear you're looking for work as a grant writer?"

Amalia smiled and nodded.

"Yes, ma'am. Did you get my resume?"

"I did. Very impressive." She paused. "You understand, though, that we have no money for new staff, right?"

"Yes."

"So your position would have to be self-funded."

"Yes, ma'am, I understand. I wrote half a dozen successful grant proposals during my short time with my last employer. I'm confident I can do the same for you here."

Kendra nodded. "I like your attitude. How do you plan to support yourself while you work on your first round of grant proposals?"

"I have some savings and a good line of credit. That should get me through the first few weeks easy. Maybe longer if I can stay here on a cot or—"

Kendra held up a hand, interrupting Amalia.

"Now, we're not set up for long term housing. But I can offer you the same thing we're offering all the Miami folks. Two weeks on the cots, with the promise that you'll spend some time volunteering in the local community. And that wouldn't include your grant writing. It would mean cooking, cleaning, doing odds and ends for other local community groups I send you to."

Amalia nodded. "I can do that."

"Good. One last question, then. Why New Orleans? Why Algiers? Why not just hop on the next bus out of town and try to find gainful employment in some city that's not on the coast? The way things are going with these storms, and all this sea level rise, New Orleans may be the next Miami. It could all go under any day now and we could all be on a bus out of here next week."

"Oh, that's exactly why I want to stay, ma'am. After what I saw in Miami, my first thought was to get as far from the coast as I could. Maybe make my way to the mountains. Colorado, maybe. But where's the sense in that? We're all connected. If the coasts fall, we all fall. So I may as well stay by the coast and do what I can to help. They're not letting anyone back into Miami right now, so this is the next best thing. I could've ended up on a bus to some other city, but I didn't. Maybe this is God's way of telling me I need to stay on the coast and keep working for climate justice."

Kendra laughed. "Maybe it is. Alright, Amalia, let's give this a try. You're going to need to find some big grant, though, to get your foot in the door. Achievable, but big."

"I will, ma'am."

"Good. Stop by my office sometime to fill out some paperwork and talk details. In the meantime, happy hunting."

———●———

Amalia sat with a few other volunteers in the dining area of the Algiers Climate Justice Center, hunched over slightly as she stared at her tablet and typed on her keyboard. She didn't want to waste money on buying a new laptop until she was more settled, but she'd managed to find a scuffed-up tablet at a nearby second-hand store and a small wireless keyboard gathering dust in a closet at the center. It wasn't an ideal setup, but it was enough for her needs. She could send email, read calls for proposals, do basic research, and write up her own grant proposals without much difficulty.

She was in the middle of working on a major grant proposal when someone came in from the main office.

"Alright, volunteers! We need everyone we can get to help with the workday over at the community garden up in the Ninth Ward. We'll be doing some gardening and taking some food over to one of the other refugee sites. Meet me at the van out front in ten minutes!"

Amalia sighed. She liked gardening and volunteering, but she really wanted to finish this grant proposal before her two weeks on the cot were up. That only left her about two days, depending on how strict Kendra was with the deadline. She saved her document, tucked her keyboard and tablet in her backpack, and headed out of the dining room.

———— ◉ ————

On Amalia's fourteenth night at the center, the building was much darker and quieter than it had been on the first night. The whirring air conditioning had become a familiar lullabye, and most of the other climate refugees from Miami had left over the course of the past two weeks, including whoever had been coughing throughout the night. A single row of lights was on near the windows at the front of the building, but everything else was dark and quiet.

Everything, that is, except for Amalia's tablet.

Amalia was lying in her cot with tablet in hand, her face bathed in the dim glow of the screen, which was set to the lowest brightness setting. She tapped and swiped the screen periodically, reviewing the

final details of her most important grant proposal. She had completed
a full draft a few hours ago, but still wanted to review the details one
more time before her meeting with Kendra in the morning.

For over an hour, she poured over the proposal and supporting
documents, making minor changes as she went. Eventually, the warmth
of her blanket and the soft whir of the air conditioner lulled her to
sleep.

———————•———————

"So. Tell me more about this Spread the Sunshine grant proposal."

Amalia cleared her throat and looked down at her notes on her
tablet. She was sitting across the table from Kendra Williams in the
conference room next to the main office. The other six chairs in the
room were empty, but the space still felt a bit small and confined,
with no windows and few decorations other than a large bookshelf,
a cluttered desk, and a big whiteboard full of notes from some other
meeting.

"Okay." Amalia took a deep breath, setting aside her tablet. "Spread
the Sunshine is a proposal I'd like to submit to the Fossil Fuels RICO
Fund, the fund set up to disburse the proceeds of the RICO judgment
against the fossil fuel industry. I assume you're familiar with FFRICO."

Kendra nodded. "Of course. We haven't applied yet, but then again
we don't have a full-time grant writer."

"You will if this proposal is accepted."

Kendra smiled. "True. Do continue."

"Okay. The FFRICO call for proposals is very detailed, but there
are a few key points to consider." Amalia glanced down at her tablet.
"Projects must support the transition to clean energy. Projects must
support a just transition, meaning that it helps communities that have
been harmed by climate change. And projects must be self-sustaining,
meaning the project can sustain itself after the one-time grant from
FFRICO runs out."

Kendra nodded. "Yes, that sounds about right. Now tell me more about your proposal."

"Okay. The concept is simple: build a huge solar installation that helps fund future solar installations."

Amalia picked up her tablet and synced it wirelessly with the small projector on the conference room table. The projector blinked to life, and the first slide of her presentation appeared on the blank white wall near the door. It showed a large photovoltaic system along with a column of numbers indicating costs and energy produced.

"This first solar system, which I'm calling the Solar Core, is ten times bigger than the electric needs of the nonprofit that hosts it. Ten percent of the system covers all of the energy needs of the nonprofit. The remaining ninety percent gets sold back to the grid, or a community solar project if you have one locally."

Amalia advanced to the next slide—a diagram featuring a large solar array in the center with arrows pointing outward to several smaller solar arrays.

"The proceeds from selling this extra energy all go back to Spread the Sunshine, which uses those funds to install solar on a smaller scale for several low-income households."

Amalia advanced to the next slide, which showed additional solar arrays branching off from the first ring of arrays.

"Each household gets a solar installation that provides twice what they need. These new installations all give their surplus back to Spread the Sunshine too. Which in turn lets Spread the Sunshine install even more solar. And so on. The result is a network of solar installations that grows over time without any additional funding."

Amalia picked up her tablet and closed her presentation. Kendra looked down at her own tablet, reviewing details of the grant proposal.

"So these low-income households that get solar installed. Is it just free?"

"It's need-based. The project installs the solar, and they pay a monthly fee based on income. The solar fee is much cheaper than the power bill it's replacing. And in most cases, their payments will pay for their half of the installation costs eventually. Everyone wins."

Kendra leaned back in her chair, staring down at her tablet for a few moments before continuing.

"Okay. I see two potential problems. If you can solve these problems, I'll sign off on the proposal."

Amalia's pulse quickened.

"What problems?"

"The first is that it's too big. It needs to be big, but they're going to want to see more local funding than you've planned for here. Which means you're going to have to find a few local businesses or agencies that can contribute."

"You're probably right. I can work on that."

"Good. And the second point is nonprofits. I want to see two options for new projects—low-income households and nonprofits. The financing for nonprofits will be different, so you'll have to work that out. But it'll strengthen your argument and might accelerate your growth."

Amalia sighed.

"I can do that. But it'll take more time."

Kendra nodded, glancing down at her tablet.

"When's the proposal due?"

"Two days."

"Oh." Kendra paused, looking off into the distance for a moment as she collected her thoughts. "Well, this proposal has a lot of promise. Why don't you stay another two days and work on the final details? You can even set aside your other volunteer duties until you submit it. How does that sound?"

Amalia's face brightened.

"That sounds great."

"Good. Keep me posted on your progress. And good luck."

———————◉———————

Amalia walked through the summer swelter with clipboard in hand, exploring unfamiliar streets in search of prospective sponsors. She was used to hot weather from growing up in Miami, but something about summertime on Louisiana's Gulf Coast felt even hotter and swampier than anything she was used to. Or maybe it just felt that way after walking city streets for five hours and talking to a dozen business owners with little to show for it.

When Amalia stepped into the used car dealership, it was mostly just to take a break from the heat. Harold's Auto wasn't on her list of likely sponsors, and the small fleet of aging gas-guzzlers parked outside didn't inspire confidence in the business's green philosophy or ability to sponsor a solar installation. But she took a deep breath, wiped the sweat off of her brow, and approached the old man sitting at a computer behind a smooth grey counter.

"Welcome to Harold's! I'm Harold, if you haven't already guessed." Harold's laughter was cheerful, but a bit loud for the small, enclosed space. "How can I help you?"

"Hi, Harold!" Amalia shook Harold's hand. "My name's Amalia. I'm a new grant writer down the street at the Algiers Climate Justice Center."

"Oh! That sounds impressive."

Amalia smiled. "Thank you. Are you familiar with the center?"

"Oh, yes." He nodded thoughtfully, glancing out the window in the general direction of the center. "I don't know much about it, but they're active in the community. Gardening and cleanups and everything. Seem like good people."

"Good." Amalia pulled one of the Spread the Sunshine handouts out of the bottom compartment of her clipboard and offered it to Harold. "We're working on a grant for a new solar energy project. It would serve as a community solar project for a few local residents or businesses who want to switch to solar. It would also help fund new solar projects."

"Oh, I see. Let's have a look."

Harold took the handout and started reading it. Amalia expected him to skim it, but he actually paused to read the full details, setting it down on the counter when he was done.

"I see. Will it include a solar charging station for cars?"

"That's a good idea, actually." Amalia wrote a quick note in the margins of the signup sheet on her clipboard. "It might. Is that something you'd be interested in?"

Harold pointed out the window at his used cars.

"These old gas-guzzlers don't need any solar, now do they?"

Harold laughed. For a moment, Amalia's pulse quickened. She wondered if he was laughing at her expense.

"Um, I—"

Harold held up a hand to interrupt her.

"I'm just messing with you, kid. I ask because my daughter's going to be taking over the business in a couple of months." Harold looked out the window again, his expression growing more serious. "She didn't want to do it at first. But then we talked about it, and she decided she could do it on one condition."

"What condition?"

"Selling off all the gas guzzlers and switching to a 100% electric auto shop."

Amalia's eyes widened.

"Oh! Thats..."

Harold laughed. "Yeah, that's about what my reaction was when she suggested it. But I looked into it, and there's nothing like it around here. Some new electric auto shops popping up over the river, but nothing around here for all the people who want a second-hand electric they can afford. Harold's Auto will be the first!"

Amalia smiled and nodded.

"Sounds like a good idea."

"You bet it is. Only the best for my daughter." Harold glanced at Amalia's clipboard and handout. "So tell me about your good idea, kid. You're running around town in the middle of a heat wave looking for something. What's the next step of this solar project of yours?"

"Well, we're looking for a few local businesses to sponsor the project. We're working on a grant, but some of the funding has to be local."

"I see."

Harold paused, looking over the handout again. Eventually, he picked up one of his business cards from the counter and handed it to Amalia.

"I tell you what. Email me all the details. I'll look it over with my daughter and see what we can come up with. I can't make any promises until I talk it over with her. But it sure would be convenient to have some solar charges a block or two away from the best second-hand electric shop in New Orleans."

Amalia smiled.

"Thank you, Harold."

"Oh, don't thank me yet until it's official. But I wish you the best of luck."

———— ◉ ————

Amalia crossed her fingers, said a silent prayer, and pressed the shiny green "Submit" button. Once the confirmation page appeared, she sighed, setting aside her tablet and leaning back in her chair with a nervous laugh.

She had finally submitted the grant proposal—a full eleven hours before the midnight deadline. Of course, there was no guarantee that her proposal would be approved. But she had put it all together, found the local support, made the necessary revisions, and submitted it all just under the wire.

Now all she could do was wait.

In the meantime, there was still plenty to do. Amalia tucked her tablet in her backpack and headed to the dining area to help with post-lunch cleanup. After cleaning tables, washing dishes, and sweeping, she headed out the door to continue her search for a permanent place to live.

She knew it wouldn't be easy given the fact that she wasn't the only new climate refugee, and there were only so many cheap studio apartments or roommate situations in all of New Orleans. But she had a good feeling about this grant, this climate justice center, and this city on the edge of the rising seas.

It wouldn't be easy—but she would find a way.

Tales from the Edge

"Some of the local farms survived the Collapse. We're still working on starting and expanding gardens in town, but we've always had farms nearby. Farms, orchards, wineries, breweries. We even have some cattle to the south."

Green Flourish
Proposal Four
The Green Aces
The Long Walk To The Capitol
Breathless

Green Flourish

Ramona Bedelia stared at the green cork leather mask cradled in her hands. She traced her fingers lightly across the smooth inner surface, turning it over slowly to explore the texture of the exterior. The deep grooves and sharp transitions between various shades of neon and hunter green created the illusion that the mask was made of oak and holly leaves. The glass-covered eye holes were crafted to fit snugly along the contours of her face, allowing for maximum visibility with minimum revelation of identity.

She closed her eyes, took one last slow breath, and slid on the mask.

The world around her didn't look any different. The thick glass lenses protecting her eyes were clear, so her sky blue walls and oak desk looked the same as they always had.

But she looked different. One look at the full-length mirror across the room changed everything. She was covered head to toe in cork leather, a leather alternative sustainably harvested from the bark of the cork oak tree. Her cork leather jacket, pants, and boots were all a matching kelly green. She slid on her green cork leather gloves and her costume was complete.

She had finally become the Green Flourish.

It was three a.m. on a Sunday morning. Harsh halogen floodlights illuminated the three acre clearing at the end of the winding country road. The fracking well pad and its assortment of trucks and trailers and drilling equipment were at least as brightly lit as any mall parking lot in the city. The surrounding woods and fields, however, were completely dark beneath the moonless sky. The floodlights pierced through the darkness immediately surrounding the dusty well pad, casting jagged shadows and bathing the trunks of trees and stalks of corn in a perpetual dusk of electric light.

Green Flourish crouched in the woods near the edge of the well pad. Intellectually, she knew that someone standing beneath those bright lights wouldn't be able to see very far into the shadows beyond the tree line. Even so, her pulse raced as she approached the edge of the woods near the front entrance of the well pad. After taking a few deep breaths to steady herself, she pulled something out of her backpack and tossed it into the air.

The small black quadcopter hummed to life, quietly floating upward and hovering about a hundred feet above the road. Green Flourish kept her eyes on the well pad for several heartbeats, watching for any signs that someone had seen her deploy the surveillance drone. When she was confident that no one was coming, she pulled out her phone and looked at the feed from the drone.

The well pad was very quiet. She could hear the hum of the generators running the lights and possibly other equipment, but the drone's aerial view showed that no one was currently walking around or working outside. As planned, she'd caught the crew in a lull between drilling the well and starting the fracking.

But she knew that she shouldn't get reckless. She probably wasn't alone.

Green Flourish stepped out of the woods, quickly crossing the several yards between the tree line and the rough dirt around the edges of the well pad. This was a small enough operation that there were no big gates or fences around the perimeter, just lines of vehicles and occasional wide gaps between them. Within moments, she was walking unnoticed among the trucks and trailers beneath the full glare of the halogen floodlights.

She pulled out two cans of spray paint, one in each hand, and started spraying. A little graffiti wouldn't do much to deter the frackers, but it might make the story go viral. After all, she was the Green Flourish now; her merry mischief should include at least a moment of artistic flourish.

After spray painting climate slogans, drawings of solar panels, and the words "Green Flourish" on each of the nearest trailers, she put away the spray cans and checked her phone to be sure that she still hadn't been spotted. No one else was in sight, so she walked out into the open.

The drilling rig was only about ten yards away, but it felt like a very long walk. Green Flourish held her head high as she walked, striding briskly but confidently toward the generators near the drilling rig. She pulled out a pair of bolt cutters and clipped the padlock on the gate of the six foot tall chain link fence that stood between her and the generators.

"Hey! What the hell are you doing over there?"

Green Flourish dropped the bolt cutters and turned around slowly, taking a slight step backward through the open gate. A burly middle-aged man in a windbreaker and blue jeans was storming across the small stretch of ground between them, pointing and glaring at her.

"I said what in the hell are you doing here, hippie! You are trespassing on private property. Put your hands—"

Green Flourish lunged to the side, reaching into a pouch on her leg and tossing a small sphere on the ground at the man's feet. The smoke bomb exploded with a sudden flash and burst of smoke, catching the man off guard. He stumbled forward through the smoke, coughing into one hand and fumbling through his pockets with another.

She didn't wait around to see what he was reaching for. She spun around and rushed toward the generators, reaching into her backpack as she ran. Running at a full sprint, she slapped a small disc onto the side of each of the four generators. When she saw that there was no exit in the fence past the generators, she made a sharp turn and ran around behind them, making her way back toward the front gate.

Where the man was waiting for her.

"Freeze!" He raised his gun and pointed it at her chest. "I swear to God I will shoot you dead!"

For a moment, Green Flourish froze. She raised her hands in the air slowly. The look of panic on the man's face softened into a smirk.

"Yeah, that's what I thought. You keep your hands where—"

Green Flourish lunged to the side. The man reflexively fired in response to the sudden motion, but she was already out of the way. She sprinted past the generators again, this time running toward the fence at full speed. She leapt into the air, grabbing the top of the fence and flipping her legs over it in one swift motion. The man behind her took aim as she landed on her feet on the other side—but when he noticed what she had placed on the generators, he lowered his gun and fled in the other direction.

Once Green Flourish was out of sight of the man with the gun, she didn't look back. She sprinted to the edge of the woods, then slowed her pace to a jog to make sure that she didn't run into any trees or branches. After looking around for a few moments, she figured out where she was and hurried toward the electric motorcycle she'd hidden nearby beneath some branches. While she was busy uncovering the bike, a series of thunderous explosions shook the well pad and surrounding woods and fields. The bright lights suddenly went out, replaced by the flickering orange glow of flames in the distance.

Green Flourish pulled her black and neon green bike out of the woods and rolled it onto the winding country road. She put on her helmet, hopped onto the seat, turned the electric engine on with a flick of her wrist, and sped off into the night.

———— ◉ ————

"I did it."

Ramona was wearing one of her typical work outfits: black pantsuit and kelly green blouse with her shoulder-length black hair back in a tight ponytail. The woman sitting next to her, Miriam, had short gray hair and wore a blue and orange sweatshirt and sweatpants. They sat together eating homemade sandwiches on a bench in the park.

"I saw something in the news yesterday that reminded me of our recent conversations. Was that you?"

"Probably."

"In Union County?"

Ramona looked around to make sure that no one was listening.

"Yes."

The two women ate together in silence for a few moments. Ramona knew better than to push for a response. Eventually, Miriam spoke.

"You're all right?"

"Yes."

"And no one was hurt?"

"Yes. I mean yes, no one was hurt."

"Good."

There was another long silence. Miriam finished her sandwich, then tucked the empty reusable container into her cloth lunch bag. As the silence continued, Ramona eventually lost her patience and spoke.

"Is that it? No praise or condemnation? You usually have more to say."

"It's not my place to judge, Ramona. I present my students with a variety of perspectives on environmental ethics. It's up to each of them to develop their own perspective and choose how to apply it in their daily lives."

"And what do you think of my perspective?"

"I understand it without embracing or condemning it. We've talked at length about your ethical framework. Destroying property in order to save lives makes perfect sense within that framework. Given the dire threat posed by global warming and the personal losses you've suffered, I find your ethical argument compelling. Of course, there isn't a court of law in the land that would agree. And the strategic value of such actions is debatable. But I understand."

"From an ethical perspective, does it matter if a court of law agrees?"

"That depends on your ethical framework."

"True."

Miriam placed her palm lightly on the back of Ramona's hand.

"Be careful out there, Ramona. I mean that in both the physical sense and the ethical sense. Some of history's greatest servants of the public good have broken the law in the pursuit of justice. But so have many of history's villains. Once you decide that you're above the law, it's easy to lose your way."

Ramona sighed. "I may already be losing my way, Miriam. I'm only one action in and I'm already hooked. The adrenaline rush is amazing. I feel like one night out in the field accomplishes so much more than a whole year of petitions and lobbying. But what if I take this thing too far?"

Miriam paused, letting Ramona's words linger before replying. "It's good that you're questioning yourself. When you stop questioning yourself, you've lost your way."

"Good point." Ramona looked down at her phone. "I've got to get back to work. But thank you for meeting with me today."

"Any time, my dear. Be careful out there."

The two women stood up and hugged each other, then went their separate ways.

———————⊙———————

Ramona's home office had minimalist furnishings: sky blue walls, a simple oak desk, a black executive office chair, and an oak bookcase filled with hardback and paperback books. After a long day at work, Ramona walked into the office and stood in front of the bookcase with a slight smile. She picked out two paperbacks: "Raising Kane" with a solid forest green cover and "Watchmen" with a yellow and black smiley face cover. When she put them together and placed them on the top shelf, the magnets hidden in the spines of the books triggered a quiet clicking sound. The right side of the bookcase swung slightly away from the wall, revealing a hidden compartment.

Ramona pulled open the secret door to reveal a brightly lit display case containing her Green Flourish gear: the suit, the backpack, several pouches, three quadcopter drones, a few boxes of supplies, a green phone, and a green laptop.

She picked up the laptop, closed the secret door, and walked over to her desk to start her research.

There wasn't any national news coverage of her first action yet aside from one or two environmental news sites. The local and regional stations and papers featured prominent stories about a "masked vigilante" who had destroyed thousands of dollars worth of property and tagged some trailers with "his" name. She was annoyed by the universal assumption that these reporters made about her sex and gender. Was it because of her decidedly unrevealing costume? Or did they just assume that anyone with the nerve to blow up generators and fend off security guards must be a masculine male?

After resisting the urge to post anonymous comments about sex and gender identity, she continued her research.

According to one article, a spokesperson for Transcendence Energy said that the company planned to continue their operations in the region. This wasn't the news that she was hoping for, but it didn't come as a surprise either. Given the current price of oil, it would take several such incidents to convince Transcendent that fracking was no longer profitable here. Unsurprisingly, she still had her work cut out for her.

What she did find surprising, however, was that the director of Transcendent Energy wasn't the most quoted source in these stories.

Most of the print articles and some of the TV and radio news stories featured quotes from a Dr. Ignacia Mendez of the International Prometheus Consortium. Ramona had vaguely heard of this group before—some ultra-conservative think tank heavily funded by the fossil fuel industry. Apparently, they were taking an active role in responding to the recent rise in mass demonstrations and property destructions at fossil fuels sites in the U.S. Almost every story cited a particular quote in part or in full.

"These attacks on our industrial infrastructure are acts of terrorism against the American people. Hydraulic fracturing is a form of natural gas production that offers local communities tremendous opportunities for gainful employment and improved access to safe, clean, abundant, and affordable energy. Our members take great pride in providing energy to the American people. We will not be deterred by violent Luddites who want the American people to live in poverty and darkness."

Dr. Mendez said that the IPC was offering a $10,000 reward for information leading to the capture of the Green Flourish. They also offered to provide Transcendence Energy with free consultation about security and public relations.

Ramona created a file on her laptop about the International Prometheus Consortium and started doing some preliminary research. She looked into the basic details of their operations: executive director, board of directors, funding, main office, satellite offices, and many associated details. After about a half hour of compiling and organizing information, she stood up and took a stretch break.

IPC was clearly important, but they would have to wait. First, she would continue with the local struggle against the intrusion of Transcendence Energy into her bioregion. In addition to the climate concerns, she knew plenty of people in the area and didn't want them all to get cancer or other ailments associated with fracking chemicals in the air and water.

After another two hours of online research and a few late night slices of cold pizza, she had found her next local target and gathered most of the information she needed to prepare for her next action.

As the details came together, she felt the familiar adrenaline rush. If she really wanted to, she could go right now. The site was only three hours away, just enough time to get there and do some quick sabotage before dawn.

But now was not the time for rash decisions. She had good intel, but she hadn't done any in-person recon, and she had to be more careful now that there was a bounty on her head. This action could wait at least one more night.

But how much more time did the people of this bioregion have—and the people of the world have—before it was too late?

Ramona closed her laptop with a sigh. This action would have to wait. But she was too wired to go to bed. She put away her laptop, made sure the secret door was closed, and headed outside for another late night walk.

There wasn't anything else that she could do tonight. But tomorrow night, she would be ready.

———●———

The Green Flourish slid her black and neon green motorcycle onto the blacktop. She put on her helmet, hopped onto the seat, and turned on the electric motor with a flick of her wrist. Before she took off, she paused for a moment to think about what awaited her at her destination. Then she sped off into the night. The road ahead was long and dangerous, but she hoped that at the end of it, she would find justice.

Proposal Four

Dr. Daniel Anderson stepped out of the elevator and walked down the long hallway, carefully reading the elegant black metal numbers next to the doors of each room.

The meeting hadn't even started yet and it was already defying his expectations. He had assumed that it would take place in some high-security military facility or sprawling government office complex with metal detectors and armed guards. Instead, he found himself wandering down a hallway in a relatively small office building that catered to people who wanted to rent meeting rooms and offices by the hour or day.

Eventually, he found the room he was looking for: Room 8891. Just as he was about to knock, Daniel looked through the small window on the door and noticed someone motioning for him to enter. He opened the door and stepped inside.

"Welcome, Dr. Anderson. My name is Brenda Madison. Please, have a seat."

Brenda Madison wore a loose-fitting black suit with a slim white shirt. Even though she remained seated, her excellent posture and smooth, efficient movements commanded an immediate air of authority.

Daniel took a seat at the small table. There was no furniture in the room other than the table and two chairs. There was also no paperwork, no computer, and nothing else visible except for Brenda Madison and a single sheet of paper on the table.

"Dr. Anderson—may I call you Daniel?"

Daniel nodded.

"Daniel, before we continue, I want to confirm that you're clear on the details of our agreement." She slid the sheet of paper across the table. "You will spend the next thirty days working with fellow consultants to solve problems related to your research. When your contract is complete, you will be free to go. However, you must never under any circumstances disclose anything about your consulting experience to anyone for any reason."

Daniel studied the sheet of paper. It was a simple legal contract. The wording was formal, but otherwise it was similar to what Brenda had just explained.

"You're offering me about ten times my annual salary for a month's worth of consulting. I wasn't aware that computational sociology was in such high demand. You're sure this is legal?"

Brenda smiled. "Don't worry. You'll be working under the supervision and direction of the United States Intelligence Community."

"That doesn't answer my question."

Brenda's smile tightened. "Legal counsel will be available throughout the duration of your contract. If you're having second thoughts—"

Daniel raised a hand to interrupt her. "No, it's alright. That's good enough for me. I'm ready to sign."

Brenda pulled a stainless steel pen out of the inner pocket of her suit coat and handed it to Daniel. After skimming the contract one last time, he signed it.

Suddenly, the door behind Daniel burst open. Before he could turn around, someone grabbed him from behind and held him in place. Someone else slipped a blindfold over his eyes. Strong hands lifted him to his feet and guided him out into the hallway.

Daniel didn't know how long it had been since he'd been taken off the helicopter and led to his current location. Standing blindfolded in an unfamiliar room had altered his perception of the passage of time. It felt like he'd been there for hours, but it had probably only been ten or twenty minutes. He didn't know much about where he was, but he knew that he wasn't alone. The room was very quiet, but he could hear the sound of other people breathing, punctuated by the occasional cough or rustling of someone moving nearby.

Eventually, someone removed his blindfold.

He was in a large conference room with about two dozen other people. Brenda Madison was standing behind a long wooden table surrounded by very comfortable-looking leather office chairs. She was accompanied by several men armed with assault rifles and covered from head to toe in black tactical gear. Daniel looked around and noticed that he was standing with his back to the wall in a row with over a dozen other people dressed in casual civilian clothing.

"Welcome, consultants. I apologize for the dramatic induction protocol. Since you're all on thirty day contracts, it was necessary to ensure that you know as little as possible about this facility. Please, have a seat."

Daniel and his fellow consultants approached the table, glancing cautiously around the room as they took their seats. The off-white walls and light blue industrial carpet gave the room a comfortable, if somewhat impersonal, look and feel. Daniel had been half-expecting to find himself in an abandoned warehouse, though, so the accommodations seemed reassuring by contrast.

"Welcome. Now that you're all here, I can provide you with more details about Operation Ammit."

Brenda pulled a phone out of her pocket and tapped the screen. A segment of the wall behind her slid silently to the side, revealing a wide-screen TV.

"For the next thirty days, you will be part of an international interdisciplinary effort to formulate rapid and decisive solutions to the global climate crisis."

A graph appeared on the screen. Daniel wasn't sure if he'd seen this particular graph before, but the information looked familiar. The graph illustrated several greenhouse gas emissions scenarios and the amount of warming that was likely to occur in each scenario.

"I know what you're thinking. Aren't people already working on this? Wasn't I already working on research related to the climate crisis?"

A new graph appeared on the screen. This graph showed a single emissions scenario that closely matched the second-highest scenario from the previous graph.

"According to our analysis, all current efforts to reduce global emissions will fail. Yes, the international community is starting to make progress. Yes, the COP21 and COP22 conferences have led to about a decade of significant improvement over the 'business as usual' scenario. But it will all be too little, too late. And failure has consequences."

The next graph was titled "Mortality: Actual and Projected, 2000-2100." It was a line graph with different lines indicating different causes of death: disease, war, famine, natural disaster, and several other labels. All of the lines rose dramatically around the year 2050, then dropped precipitously thereafter.

"In my first draft of this presentation, I included dozens of more nuanced graphs that were used in the development of this mortality projection. The graphs showed an increase in extreme droughts, floods, and wildfires. The graphs showed a decline in land ice and the accelerating collapse of the Western Antarctic Ice Sheet. The graphs showed the thawing of Arctic permafrost and resultant release of incredible quantities of methane into the atmosphere within just the past few years.

"But at the end of the day, the reason we've organized Operation Ammit and hired you as consultants is summed up in this single graph.

After an extensive analysis conducted by thousands of our top security analysts, we've concluded with a high degree of confidence that the mortality rate will skyrocket sometime around 2050 due primarily to consequences of anthropogenic global warming. This will result in the sudden death of most human beings and the collapse of global civilization as we know it."

Daniel stared at the graph in stunned silence. Brenda paused, giving her audience time to absorb the gravity of the situation.

"This is the future as it stands. Over the next thirty days, you will identify the best solutions to change that future. You will analyze a broad array of action proposals and formulate your own proposals according to our guidelines. At the end of thirty days, we will implement the best of these proposals as soon as possible."

Brenda tapped her phone to advance to the next image. Daniel was expecting another graph, but it was a close-up shot of a military drone in mid-flight in a clear blue sky.

"Let me be very clear. When I say action, I'm not talking about signing a petition. You are now part of an elite team of consultants hand-picked by senior members of the United States Intelligence Community. Your mission is to determine which courses of action are most likely to avert the collapse of global civilization. This goal must be achieved by any means necessary. You are not to impose your own moral or ethical perspectives on your analysis of proposals. You must simply use your expertise in your field to assist in the development of effective and reliable solutions."

Brenda tapped her phone again. The wall panel slid back in front of the monitor.

"There will be no questions at this time. We will distribute your first round of proposals in ten minutes. In the meantime, I encourage you to get to know each other. Restrooms and light snacks will be available once you've received your proposals. Thank you."

Brenda turned away from the table and walked out the door. Several of Daniel's fellow consultants stood up and started asking questions, but Brenda ignored them. Daniel was too lost in thought to join their questioning. As he watched Brenda leave the room, his mind was finally able to focus on a single thought.

He was starting to get the impression that this was going to be an interesting thirty days.

⸻ ◉ ⸻

Hundreds of sheets of paper were scattered across the conference table. The consultants had clustered into small groups of three or four people, occasionally circulating around the room to ask questions or switch groups. Some were taking notes or doing back-of-the-envelope calculations on the legal pads and black tablets that had been provided along with the proposals.

Daniel was in the midst of a conversation with an eclectic group of thinkers: a historical climatologist named Hiwot, an environmental economist named Edith, and a futurist named Fatin. He studied the table of contents of the proposal packet, writing a few notes in the margins as the discussion continued.

"How about if we review the proposals again in order? We can do a quick review of all ten followed by a more careful analysis of the top two or three."

Edith shook her head. "I don't want to waste any more time on the more violent proposals. Why did they even put those in there? Do they really expect us to recommend a campaign of wars and assassinations? It sounds like World War Three."

"It already is World War Three." Hiwot paged through the proposal packet as she spoke. "I don't like the more militant proposals either, but I understand why they're there. It's all happening too fast. We warned the world about the collapsing Western Antarctic Ice Sheet, the Arctic methane release, and all the other abrupt climate change scenarios that were mostly hypothetical at the time. But nobody listened. Now that so many of them are actually happening, the whole world's unraveling. Proposals Two through Six look particularly ugly—but they're not as bad as what will happen if we do nothing."

Edith raised her hands as if to fend off Hiwot's rebuttal. "I know, I know. Don't misunderstand me. I'm not underestimating the severity of the situation. I'm just questioning the efficacy of violence in solving the problem. Governments always want to solve problems through government intervention—and violence is the nastiest of all government interventions."

"And what's your solution? Let the markets sort it out? How well has that worked historically?"

Edith raised her hands defensively again. "Now, now. I'm not advocating a purely market-based approach. But there are sensible market interventions that would be highly effective at disincentivizing fossil fuel consumption. An evidence-based, revenue-neutral carbon tax, for example."

Fatin nodded. "Yes. Proposal Eight includes such a carbon tax as the central component of full set of economic interventions. That's arguably the strongest proposal so far. But I still see value in analyzing all proposals. The best solution will likely involve a bundle of seemingly unrelated small solutions that work together synergistically to create a smoother transition to a zero-carbon economy and rapid adaptation to the most severe consequences of anthropogenic global warming."

The group fell silent for a few moments, reflecting on Fatin's words. Eventually, he spoke again.

"Daniel, you've been quiet. What do you think?"

Daniel took a deep breath, gathering his thoughts. "Two things. First of all, I agree that we should analyze all of the proposals in depth. If we don't like the violent ones—which seems to be the case, at least in our small group—then we can say why, in strategic rather than ethical terms, these violent solutions won't work. Deeper than that, though, my biggest concern right now is modeling. How are we going to model all of this? I sure as hell hope they've got some supercomputers and a team of analysts stashed away somewhere. If we want to back up our off-the-cuff conjecture with serious analysis and complex modeling, we're going to need more than a few legal pads and cheap tablets."

Everyone nodded in agreement. Daniel smiled, picking up his proposal packet and pen as he continued.

"Alright. Now that I've gotten that off my chest, let's get back to these proposals. How about if we keep it simple and start with Proposal One?"

———————◉———————

The cafeteria looked as nondescript and institutional as the rest of the compound: off-white walls, blue industrial carpeting, a long marble counter between the dining area and kitchen, simple yet elegant plastic folding tables and stackable padded chairs. There were no signs, posters, decorations, or even light switches on the walls, which filled Daniel with a vaguely uneasy feeling when he stopped to think about it. Mostly, though, it all seemed uninteresting and utterly forgettable.

The food, on the other hand, was much more interesting. As Daniel approached the front of the line, he could see and smell a variety of unusual dishes. When he reached the counter, the server glanced at his name tag and turned to grab a ready-made tray of food from the kitchen.

To Daniel's surprise, it was Thai Pizza, one of his all-time favorite takeout meals.

Daniel's eyes widened.

"Is that really Thai Pizza?"

The server, a young woman in a white uniform, smiled at his question.

"Yes, sir. It's not from your usual spot off the Delmar Loop, but our master chef has done her best to recreate the recipe. We hope you'll enjoy it."

"That's amazing. How did you even know?"

The server smirked. "Trust me—they know things about you that you don't even know."

Daniel chuckled, debating if he should be laughing, or worried, or both. He took his tray of Thai Pizza and headed over to the tables to find a seat. Hiwot waved at him, so he decided to sit with her.

"What is that? Gourmet pizza?"

"Thai pizza. What did you get?"

"Chocolate milkshake and bacon cheeseburger with extra pickles. They really did their homework. It's a bit unsettling, isn't it?"

Daniel laughed. "So it's not just me then."

"No. Do you think we'll eat like this every day?"

"I don't know."

The two ate together in silence for a few minutes. The cafeteria was quiet as everyone enjoyed their favorite meal. Once Hiwot had almost finished her cheeseburger, she set it aside and spoke again.

"What do you make of all this? Do you think they're really going to do whatever we say? I mean, if we say the word, are they really going to go around assassinating and bombing people?"

Daniel shrugged. "Maybe. I'm sure they'll take our recommendations seriously. Otherwise, why are they spending so much money on this? We have to assume that what we say will at least influence their decisions."

"Good point." Hiwot took another bite of her burger. "So do you think it's even ethical to participate? It's one thing to do research like this in the halls of academia. It's another thing entirely to do it for the intelligence community."

Daniel paused, setting aside his last slice of pizza as he considered the question. "I've been wondering about that. I suppose it depends on your perspective on ethics. In a university context, I'm sure it wouldn't fly. But remember, we're not in a university context. We're here as individual human beings doing freelance consulting for government agencies. The question is, if they take our research and use it as a justification for violence, can we live with ourselves?"

"Yes, that's the question." Hiwot sighed. "Honestly, I don't know the answer. I want to say no; I want to say that we shouldn't participate. But a part of me wants to at least do the analysis."

Daniel nodded. "I agree. Maybe we can hope that the analysis will demonstrate that the most effective proposals are also the least violent."

Hiwot smiled, but her big brown eyes were heavy with sadness. "We can hope so, Daniel. We can hope so."

———◦———

Daniel awoke with a start. He sat up in bed, not remembering for a moment where he was or what restless dream had disturbed his slumber. After taking a few deep breaths, it all came back to him.

He was alone in his quarters at the compound. It was Day Twenty-Three of his contract. For the third night in a row, he'd had nightmares about Operation Ammit.

Daniel couldn't remember the details clearly, but the latest nightmare had involved a disjointed mix of climate disasters and aerial combat. The only semi-coherent memory involved walking with hundreds of people through an endless wasteland of bubbling mud and ice. He was dizzy and nauseated from inhaling the methane releasing all around him. Wave after wave of fighter jets and drones thundered through the air overhead. When he slipped and fell down in the mud, the sudden impact of the muddy ice against his face startled him awake.

He turned on the LED lamp on the nightstand and looked around. There was no one else in the room, and no one seemed to be in the small adjoining bathroom. His sense of foreboding must have just been a lingering effect of the dream.

Daniel sighed and slid out of bed. After a quick shower and breakfast in the cafeteria, he headed to Conference Room Three.

The consultants had spent the first week working together as one large group. During the second and third weeks, they had split up into two working groups. Since Daniel was one of the few consultants who had extensive experience with computerized social modeling and simulation, he was helping both groups create highly complex simulations of global responses to various proposals and scenarios.

Even with the help of an unseen network of analysts and supercomputers provided by Brenda Madison, it was a daunting task. The biggest challenge was getting models from different fields—climatological models, economic models, social models, and so on—to work together as a single global meta model. The theoretical and technical complexity of the task seemed to merit a multi-year research project rather than a thirty day intensive. However, Daniel and the others had done their best to create something preliminary to present to the full team.

After twenty-three days discussing everything from the horrors of contemporary warfare to the intricacies of computer modeling and simulation, both working groups finally had their first results.

The entire twenty-six member consulting team was gathering in Conference Room Three. Daniel had volunteered to present Team A's findings. Once everyone was seated, he cleared his throat and rose to his feet.

"Alright everyone. Let's start with the basics."

Daniel studied his notepad carefully before proceeding. The conference room was so quiet that he could hear the sound of his breathing and the rustle of paper as he turned to the proper page.

"Out of the twenty-seven proposals we reviewed, there were four that Team A was unable to model. Out of the twenty-three remaining proposals, we identified three with the highest likelihood of rapidly reducing emissions and adapting quickly enough to avoid a collapse.

Those were Proposals Eleven, Seventeen, and Four. Team B, what were your findings?"

Fatin stood up, quickly reviewing his tablet before speaking.

"Team B also couldn't model four of the proposals. They were too vague in their framing or too difficult to model so quickly. But we had a slightly different top three list: Proposals Nineteen, Fifteen, and Four."

"Okay. Thanks, Fatin. That means that the leading proposal so far is..."

Daniel's heart started racing. He looked down at his notes to confirm the title, but he already knew it without looking. He'd spent the past few weeks studying these proposals in intimate detail. This proposal in particular was one that everyone knew by heart.

"Proposal Four: Asymmetrical Global Intervention."

The conference room exploded into a cacophony of shouting. Several people jumped to their feet, raising their voices and hands in anger. Hiwot scowled and threw her notepad against the wall. Fatin sat back down, setting aside his tablet and shaking his head. Daniel just stood there watching it all in sullen silence.

Most people knew that their own team had given Proposal Four a fairly high rating, but no one knew until now that it was the lead proposal.

As the room splintered into half a dozen separate arguments, Daniel came back to his senses. He pounded on the desk and shouted for everyone's attention.

"People! Let's keep it together here. I know that this isn't the outcome we-"

"It's a disaster!" Hiwot took a deep breath, placing her hands on the table and trying to calm herself. "This is the worst option for human rights. There will be a sharp increase in drone strikes. Sabotage. Assassinations. Torture. Even on U.S. soil against U.S. citizens! All in the name of rapidly minimizing global emissions."

Edith raised her hand as if waiting to be called on. "I thought you'd like Four, Hiwot. It's basically state-sanctioned ecoterrorism. The ultimate government intervention. Isn't that what you want?"

"No!" Hiwot shook her head and waved her arms dismissively. "Look at the broad wording. It's the Patriot Act on steroids. No one will be safe. They'll go after polluters, yes, but they'll also go after activists. Anyone who allegedly threatens national security or interferes with the decarbonization process will be arrested or killed or simply disappeared. They'll probably even conduct violent attacks and blame it on the activists. It'll be-"

"Alright, everyone. We clearly have a problem here. Let's deal with this problem rationally." Daniel paged through his notes, not entirely sure what he was looking for. "Clearly, no one wants Proposal Four. This leaves us with two options. We can either take another look at the numbers, or we can include our critiques of Proposal Four in the qualitative analysis. Or we can do both. But remember, they're asking for a scientific analysis, not an ethical one. If we disagree with Proposal Four on ethical grounds-"

Hiwot interrupted. "They can ask for whatever they want, Daniel. It doesn't mean we have to do it. If we reject the ethicality of certain proposals, then we can stop analyzing those proposals. And we can all go on strike if they continue to push those military proposals. I say we take a vote and eliminate Proposal Four entirely."

The room fell silent. People looked around at each other, collecting their thoughts and wondering who would speak next. As Fatin was raising his hand and opening his mouth, Brenda Madison burst into the room, followed by a dozen guards in black tactical gear.

"Good morning, consultants! I have two very important points of information to discuss with you today."

Brenda walked over to the head of the table, motioning for everyone to sit down. A few people were slow to comply, but eventually everyone but Brenda and the guards was seated.

"First point: you've done amazing work over the past twenty-three days! You've gathered and analyzed more data than we thought possible in such a short span of time. If it were up to me, you'd each receive the Medal of Freedom. Please, give yourselves a big hand."

Brenda started clapping enthusiastically. The consultants looked around at each other and slowly started clapping along with Brenda. Three of them, including Hiwot, didn't clap.

"Second point: Operation Ammit is quite possibly the most important operation currently being conducted by any agency of the United States Intelligence Community. We need to take action to address this threat immediately. Your expertise is urgently needed in order for us to take action. Any individual—and I mean ANY individual—who willfully disrupts this operation will be subject to prosecution on charges including but not limited to sedition. Are we clear?"

Several people raised their hands. Brenda ignored them.

"Good. Thank you for your service. Good luck during the remaining seven days of your contract!"

Brenda and her guards marched out of the room. When they were gone, a long silence ensued. Eventually, Fatin was the first to speak.

"There you have it. Now that that's settled, let's do our best to develop an accurate analysis of these proposals. Hopefully we can find the right balance between our principles and the need to take decisive action to solve the problem."

———— ◉ ————

The helicopter ride home somehow seemed longer than the ride to the compound had been. Daniel wasn't sure if that was his imagination or if they were actually taking him to a different city instead of taking him home. Eventually, he was led off of the helicopter and into another building.

When the guards let go of his arms, Daniel took off his blindfold. To his surprise, he was standing in the same office where he had been recruited just one month ago. His phone, keys, and wallet were on the table in front of him. The guards who had led him into this room had already disappeared down the hall. It was almost as though the past thirty days had never happened.

Daniel took a deep breath, letting it out slowly with a long sigh. He gathered up his belongings, turned his phone on, and headed home.

***

After spending two weeks obsessively searching online for any news that might be related to his time with Operation Ammit, Daniel settled into a fairly comfortable routine.

Wake up. Jog. Shower. Turn on the TV news channels, open his laptop, and check for any Google Alerts in his inbox. If nothing obvious jumped out at him, he would go about the rest of his day as if his thirty days at the compound had never happened.

What else could he do? He had no one to talk to about the experience. He often considered reaching out to his fellow consultants. He remembered their names and could search for them online. But the contract forbade discussing the experience with anyone, including fellow consultants.

After another few weeks, Daniel had started to put the experience behind him. He wasn't teaching this semester, but he was working on a research project that demanded considerable attention. Turning on the TV in the morning started to become a background habit rather than a daily search for news.

And then it happened.

Daniel didn't even notice anything unusual when he first turned on the TV. After putting a slice of bread into his toaster, he turned on his computer and checked his email. When he saw that there were several Google Alerts, his pulse quickened. He looked over at the TV and noticed that the regular morning news had been preempted by a special report. There was a big banner at the top of the screen.

"Day of Terror: Ongoing Attacks in Multiple Cities"

The left half of the screen showed a scorched SUV and partially collapsed two-story building. The right half showed a pundit who was discussing the latest news. There was still no clear understanding of motive, but commentators had been quick to note that the attacks seemed coordinated, and all of the targets had connections to the fossil fuel industry.

As the man on the news spoke, the image on the left side of the screen kept changing to reveal more scenes of carnage: burning buildings, widespread power outages, train lines shut down by derailments or explosions. The incidents were spreading around the world in a wave, with numerous attacks in each time zone at about 8 a.m. local time. The attacks had started in Europe and spread at least as far as the East Coast.

It was currently 7:58 a.m. Central Standard Time.

Daniel started pacing back and forth in his living room. He didn't know with any certainty which proposal or proposals had been chosen. He also wasn't sure he would ever know. They had sent all of the consultants home after thirty days even though a clear consensus had not been reached. There were several proposals that involved some violence. These incidents could be a part of any one of these proposals.

Or they could be completely unrelated.

But this seemed too soon after the consulting job to be a coincidence. Daniel didn't have any military experience, but he suspected four or five weeks would have been enough time to select several locations, do reconnaissance, gather supplies, and so on.

Maybe this was an action taken directly by the government. Or maybe it was a radical response to some unknown government action. Either way, the result was the same.

Suddenly, Daniel heard a loud boom in the distance. His TV and lights all blinked out, leaving the apartment in darkness. The only light left in the room was the glow of his laptop and the sunlight peeking through the gap between his living room curtains.

Daniel's heart started pounding. He turned back to his laptop and searched for local news, but his internet connection was down. He pulled out his phone and noticed that he wasn't getting a wireless signal. Electricity, internet, and cell service were all gone.

Whatever was happening, it was the start of something new. And the more he thought about it, the more it looked like Proposal Four.

The Green Aces

"There she is, folks!"

Hundreds of people rose to their feet in the stands of Saluki Stadium. The horseshoe-shaped stadium had a seating capacity of fifteen thousand, but this gathering of a few hundred people was the largest crowd it had seen since the early days of the Collapse. Simple black sans-serif letters on the two-storey press box proclaimed the stadium to be the "HOME OF THE SALUKIS." Beneath these words, a more recent sign made out of two salvaged white vinyl banners said "WELCOME TO CARBONDALE."

"Ladies and gentlemen, I am pleased to present the Catalyst! And her infamous crew, the Green Aces!"

The crowd cheered and waved as the Catalyst made its final descent into Carbondale. It was a one-of-a-kind aircraft—a prototype solar-powered heavy-lift dirigible with a cigar-shaped envelope, four helicopter rotors on the low sides of the envelope, a large kelly green gondola, and a lightweight black cargo container attached to the bottom of each of the rotors. The top half of the envelope was covered in shiny photovoltaic solar modules, while the bottom half was a smooth surface that matched the kelly green of the gondola.

As the Catalyst approached, it soon became obvious that it would barely fit in the football stadium. If the goal posts had still been standing, they would have poked the underside of the 390-foot behemoth. The dirigible drifted to a halt a few yards above the field, maneuvering the gondola over a large X before descending to a gentle landing on the artificial turf.

The rotors slowed to a stop and the double doors of the gondola opened.

Two green electric motorcycles sped out onto the field, each pulling a small trailer filled with a stack of solar modules. The crowd burst into applause and cheers as the cycles whipped around the gondola, waving to the assembled citizens of the Free State of South Illinois as they rode in circles along the edge of the field.

A troupe of eleven dancers followed the cycles out of the gondola, tumbling and dancing their way toward the welcome platform at the far northern edge of the field. They were dressed in a curious blend of colorful corsets, waistcoats, tailcoats, top hats, gloves, goggles, and looser-fitting cloth and leather garments. The most prominent color was green, but every color of the rainbow was represented in one or more of their accents. Six of the dancers at the center of the troupe were playing musical instruments while they danced—accordion, ukulele, djembe, fiddle, electric guitar, and keytar, all amplified by the gondola's speakers.

The dancers danced and played their way up to the welcome platform beneath the broken digital scoreboard at the north end of the field. As they ascended the steps, they finished their song and bowed repeatedly to the cheering crowd before solemnly taking their spot in front of the Mayor and City Council.

"Welcome, Green Aces! My name is Samantha Henderson and I'm the Mayor of Carbondale. On behalf of myself and the City Council, I'm pleased to welcome you to the City of Carbondale and the Free State of South Illinois!"

One of the Green Aces stepped forward. She was a young woman in a forest green tailcoat, matching green pants, black boots, and a black and green top hat. Her wavy red hair flowed freely over her shoulders, a stark contrast to the angular lines and earth tones of her outfit.

"Thank you for the warm welcome! My name is Molly Fallon. I'm the captain of the Catalyst and spokesperson of the Green Aces. It's a pleasure to be here in the Free State of South Illinois!"

The crowd cheered and shouted and howled their welcome. Rather than trying to talk over the crowd, the Green Aces went straight into their next song. The entire stadium and surrounding landscape echoed with their music, cheers, and laughter.

———————●———————

Mayor Henderson, Molly, and half a dozen of the other Green Aces were lounging around in a circle of old-fashioned plastic lawn chairs spread out near the open double doors of the Catalyst's gondola. The rest of the Green Aces had gone into town to distribute solar panels and explore the city of Carbondale. Those who stayed behind for the meeting were listening to a playlist of pre-Collapse music on the gondola's sound system and passing around a heaping plate of homemade pot brownies. The sun was slowly setting in the west, casting the faces around the circle in shades of twilight.

"That was quite an entrance."

Molly laughed. "Yes, quite."

"Do you always make an entrance like that?"

"On a good day. Most days, I might add, are good ones."

Molly took one of the brownies and passed the plate to Mayor Henderson. The mayor smiled, passing the brownies to the next Green Ace in the circle without taking one.

"What's that all about? Trying to make a good impression on the locals?"

"Oh, I've always had a flair for the dramatic." Molly smirked, finishing her brownie as she spoke. "But it's not just that. The people need inspiration! All of the adults and most of the children have been alive long enough to watch an entire world crash and burn. Floods, droughts, wars, famines, whole cities lost to the sea. The climate apocalypse was harder on some than others, but we've all done our time—starving half to death in some FEMA camp or hiding out in the woods for Goddess knows how long. What a dreary world, right?"

"Right."

"Wrong!" Molly leapt to her feet, clapping her hands together with a twinkle in her eyes. "We live in an amazing world! A world of fabulous opportunity. A world of overflowing abundance, even after all we've done to ravage and ruin it. We Green Aces sing and dance everywhere we go so that the people will know there's still hope! The sun still shines, the wind still blows, and there are still acres upon acres of land where the food still grows. If we can gather our wits and put in the work, we may yet find our way back to the Garden."

Mayor Henderson nodded. "Yes. I like it. That's exactly the kind of spirit we could use here in Carbondale."

"You and half the world!" Molly laughed. "That's what we're here for. We only stay a little while, but we aim to leave each place in better shape than we found it. Between the—what, thirteen of us now?—we've got just about enough skills to start a new settlement from scratch. Add in all the skills that your local people have, and I'm sure we'll get this town up to speed in no time."

"Thank you." The mayor breathed a sigh of relief. "How can we ever repay you? All we have is our local currency and not much to offer in trade."

"Oh, I'm sure we'll figure out something." Molly smiled, dismissing the mayor's concerns with a wave of her hand. "The folks in the big cities are hard at work trying to reassemble the well-oiled economic machine that nearly tore this world to pieces. But the Aces operate on bit of a gift economy. Give us food and drink while we're here, and humor us if we have any random requests for goods and services. You never know what junk you have lying around that the next town over needs."

"Yes, by all means. So where do we start?"

"Consultation. Tell us more about your problems and we'll see what we can do to fix them. More often than not, all it takes is a fresh perspective. If there's work that needs to be done, we'll stick around a few weeks to get it started. The rest is up to you."

Mayor Henderson nodded. "Alright. Let's start with the basics then. Let's start with food."

———◦———

The searing September sun shined on the two acre urban garden and everyone in it. The air was heavy with a sweltering humidity so thick that sweat refused to evaporate, clinging tenaciously to the clothes and bodies of the gardeners.

Most of the two dozen gardeners were locals—lean young women and men in T-shirts, halter tops, jeans shorts, full-length jeans, and heavy work gloves. They were clearly no strangers to manual labor, working hard at a steady pace in spite of the punishing heat. Mayor Henderson was the oldest among them in her mid-thirties, but she still kept pace with her younger companions. The gardeners harvested summer fruits and vegetables, pulled weeds, turned compost, and dug new rows in preparation for fall and winter gardens.

The five Green Aces stood out among the gardeners. They also wore shirts and mostly shorts, but a few wore loose-fitting off-white poet shirts accented with rainbow-colored ribbons and scarves and gloves. Molly wore a green top hat, black cargo shorts, black gloves, and a green and black bikini top.

"You Carbondale folks sure know how to work!"

Mayor Henderson paused in her shoveling, wiping the sweat from her brow.

"Most people who survived the Collapse do. I'm impressed with how well your Aces are keeping up! I thought maybe you just spent all day singing and dancing."

Molly laughed.

"Work hard, play hard. That's what I say."

The gardeners worked together until dusk. As the sun met the treeline, the western horizon lit up in the fiery oranges and reds of an early autumn sunset. The garden and its gardeners were cast in a golden glow. As they started packing up their tools and heading for the tool shed, a pedal-powered tricycle pulled up to the field with a small trailer in tow. Mayor Henderson walked over to greet the new arrival.

"Cider time!"

The cyclist hopped out of her seat and opened up the two large coolers she was carrying in her trailer.

Molly's eyes widened. She turned to the mayor in disbelief.

"Hard cider? Cold?"

"Yes! Cold, hard, and local. Made in Southern Illinois since before the Collapse."

"Now it's my turn to be impressed."

Mayor Henderson laughed. The mayor and a few of her friends started passing the cool amber bottles around to their fellow gardeners, including the Green Aces. After opening their bottles and taking a few drinks, they all fell back into casual conversation.

Molly took a long drink and looked out over the garden.

"You've got a few good gardens here in town. Some towns we visit don't have much at all. They're still scavenging cans and trading for fresh food. This is a good start. And I hear you have a few farms to the south?"

"Yes. Some of the local farms survived the Collapse. We're still working on starting and expanding gardens in town, but we've always had farms nearby. Farms, orchards, wineries, breweries. We even have some cattle to the south. We've got a good trade network going. Murphysboro, Carterville, even some trade with Anna now."

"But not Marion."

An uneasy silence settled over the group at Molly's mention of the town of Marion. After considerable thought, the mayor spoke.

"Marion had it rough during the Collapse. There were just too many refugees from Chicago looking for food and shelter. A lot of them walked three hundred miles with nothing but the clothes on their back and a few basic supplies. Town after town told most of them to keep on walking. By the time they got to Marion, they were desperate. And Marion wasn't in the mood for visitors. It didn't end well."

"But Marion's still around?"

"Oh, yes." Mayor Henderson looked to the eastern horizon. "They're about an hour and a half to the east by bicycle. Half hour or less by truck. The road's still good, but they don't take kindly to visitors. There's a roadblock where Route 13 meets Route 148."

A young man in a blue T-shirt and jeans stepped forward and spoke.

"The raids. Tell her about the raids, Sam."

"We don't know that it's them, Tom. It could be any-"

Tom raised a hand to interrupt. "I grew up in Marion. I recognized a few of the men who raided the Wal-Mart. These men would take Carbondale by force if they thought they could hold it."

The mayor shook her head. "But it's not the whole city, Tom. That's what I'm saying. It's a few loose cannons, not the Marion city council. And we have our loose cannons here in Carbondale too. Remember what all happened here during the Collapse."

The group once again fell silent. Molly took the opportunity to finish her cider and jump back into the conversation.

"So there have been armed raids on Carbondale?"

Mayor Henderson nodded. "Yes. It's mostly been raids on our eastern and southern trade routes. But lately they've started hitting houses and storefronts on the far east side of town. No fatalities yet, thank God. But this can't go on forever." She sighed. "Didn't we learn anything from the Collapse? Four billion gone in a single generation. Flood, drought, famine, war. I thought everyone left had learned the value of cooperation. But not these raiders."

"Some people are slow learners. Old habits die hard."

Molly looked around at her fellow Green Aces. They all anticipated her question and nodded in unspoken agreement. The smile returned to Molly's face as she turned back to the mayor.

"Sam, it would be our pleasure to pay a visit to Marion. We could inquire about these raids and try to negotiate trade if the locals are friendly. How does that sound?"

The mayor smiled, breathing a sigh of relief. "That sounds wonderful, Molly. Thank you. But isn't it too dangerous? They've got armed guards posted on the road into Marion."

"Roads?" Molly grinned, pulling her goggles down over her eyes. "Where we're going, we don't need roads."

———————◆———————

The Catalyst drifted down into a grassy field next to the runway at Williamson County Regional Airport. It would have been a very small airport by big city standards—two perpendicular runways, a small taxiing area, and a few small buildings and parking lots between the runways and the highway. Given the current state of most larger airports, however, it was an impressive sight to the crew of the Catalyst.

Almost as impressive as the growing number of pickup trucks, sedans, and armored personnel carriers pouring out onto the fields and runways around the shiny green and black dirigible landing uninvited on the western edge of Marion territory.

By the time the Catalyst touched ground, the dirigible was completely surrounded by pre-Collapse vehicles. The revving and humming of dozens of federally outlawed internal combustion engines competed with the loud whirring of the Catalyst's four rotors. Armed men and women stepped out of their vehicles and took aim at the gondola, rotors, and envelope of the dirigible. As the rotors slowed to a stop, the gondola's speakers repeated their pre-recorded message.

"We come in peace. We are on a mission of peace and humanitarian aid. Please accept our apologies for our unexpected arrival. We look forward to meeting you."

After a few more repetitions, the message stopped. The gondola doors slowly swung open. Two Green Aces with large white flags on bamboo flagpoles emerged from the dirigible. They stood on either side of the gondola doors and held them open.

Molly stepped out of the gondola. She was wearing a neon green sundress, black ballistic vest, black boots, and a black and green top hat. She walked out of the gondola with her hands over her head, clutching a large paper road map of Illinois in her left hand.

"Hello? Is this Marion?"

Dozens of men and women pointed their weapons at Molly. Some of them were wearing full camouflage uniforms and wielding assault rifles. Some wore police uniforms and drove police cars. Others were dressed in civilian clothes—mostly T-shirts and jeans, though a few wore button-up shirts.

Molly took a few cautious steps forward. She stopped several yards away from the gondola, slowly waving at the armed welcoming committee with a sheepish grin.

"Hi everyone. We're looking for the city of Marion. Can I speak to someone in charge?"

A sleek black Hummer sped up to the gondola, stopping just a few yards short of Molly. The man who stepped out of the driver's side door wore a gray suit, red tie, and black ballistic armor similar to Molly's. The other men who emerged from his vehicle were carrying assault rifles which they promptly pointed at Molly.

"I'm in charge. I'm the mayor of Marion—and you've got about thirty seconds to explain what you're doing in my city."

"Oh!"

Molly's eyes widened and her jaw dropped as she did her best impression of a deer caught in the headlights. The surprising number of deadly weapons pointed at her made it easier than usual to play the part of a harmless lost traveler. She showed her road map to the mayor, pointing to a spot on the map and taking a few slow steps forward.

"I'm sorry, Mr. Mayor. We were just following Illinois Route 13 east to U.S. Route 57. We thought we could stop in Marion for rest and trade."

"Route 13's closed. Route 57's closed. Marion's closed."

"Isn't 57 an interstate route? Free travel among free states?"

The mayor laughed. "Ma'am, as you may have noticed, the federal government is not what it used to be. Nor is the State of Illinois. Now, I'd suggest you-"

"I respect your autonomy, Mr. Mayor." Molly's expression and tone gradually became more confident and firm. "But can't we spend just one afternoon in your lovely town? We just want to recharge our batteries in this sunny field and see if anyone wants to do any trading. We can even put on a free show if you'd like. We'll be gone by sunset. Honest."

The mayor took a good long look at Molly and the gondola of the Catalyst. Eventually, he let out a long sigh.

"Are your people armed?"

She hesitated, reading the man's expression carefully before responding.

"No guns. Just a few tools. Hammers, saws, knives. We sometimes work construction or farming."

"Will you submit to an inspection?"

Molly hesitated again. "If you insist."

"We do. And you'll leave by sundown?"

"If you want us to, then yes."

"Alright. Assuming you pass inspection, you can stay." He pointed at the gondola. "But I want you out of here by sunset. We're not looking to take in any more refugees. And you need to answer a few more questions."

"Yes, sir. Sounds like a good deal. Thank you, Mr. Mayor."

"Mayor Robertson. You can call me Burt."

"Thank you, Burt."

"And you are?"

"Molly. Molly Fallon."

"Pleased to meet you, Molly. Welcome to Marion."

The Green Aces were decked out in some of their finest performance outfits—an eclectic collection of corsets and waistcoats and the like, similar but not identical to what they'd worn for their performance in Carbondale. The high school football stadium seats had almost as many people as the Green Aces had seen in the Carbondale stadium. It was an impressive turnout for such short notice.

Molly lead the first act, singing and dancing along with her companions. The people of Marion weren't nearly as enthusiastic about the performance as the people of Carbondale had been. There was a palpable tension in the air as the audience warily watched the performers, taking their time to decide what to make of the strangers. But Molly didn't find that surprising given the fact that the Green Aces had shown up in Marion unannounced and uninvited.

After a few songs, the audience started to warm up to the performance, though some were clearly still reserving their judgment about the performers. When half of the musicians set down their instruments and started an elaborate juggling routine, Molly slipped away from the group and made her way out of the stadium.

Mayor Robertson was standing in the parking lot near his black Hummer. He was still wearing his heavy ballistic vest, but his posture was more casual as he engaged in animated conversation with half a dozen well-dressed men and women. The small group was standing in a semi-circle around the vehicle, guarded by another half-dozen men in camouflage uniforms with assault rifles in hand.

As Molly approached, their voices fell silent. Mayor Robertson turned to greet her.

"Alright, Molly. These are a few members of our city council. We have a few questions for you."

Molly nodded to the guards and walked up to the mayor, making sure to keep her distance and not make any sudden movements.

"Sounds good. I'm ready when you are."

"Good. First question: what is your association with Carbondale?"

Molly shrugged. "We stopped there on our way here. Seemed like a nice enough place. But we're vagabonds, not bound by the limits of any one city or state."

One of the council members, a middle-aged man in a button-up short-sleeve shirt, leaned in slightly toward the Mayor.

"Ask her about the raids, Burt."

Molly's eyes widened. Mayor Robertson dismissed the other man's concern with a wave of his hand.

"I'm getting to that, Bill. Molly, we've recently had a few of our trucks on the western route raided. The raiders didn't kill anyone, but they did wound a few of our men and seize a few shipments of food and tools. Now they've escalated. Last week, they hit our machine shop. But we fought them off, thank God. We really need that machine shop."

Bill interjected again. "I'm telling you, Burt, it's Carbondale! Carbondale's full of takers. Too many Chicago transplants over there who don't even know how to grow their own food or make their own tools. So what else are they going to do? They need our food to make it through the winter. It's that simple."

Mayor Robertson shook his head. "Bill, it's not the whole city. It's just a few bad apples. There's no way the whole city would turn on us. They've re-established the rule of law there."

"But-"

Molly raised her hand to interrupt. "Alright, gentlemen. What we have here is a simple misunderstanding. One of the main reasons we came this way is because Carbondale's been raided too—and they blame Marion."

Everyone stared at her in disbelief. Even the guards, who had mostly been ignoring the conversation, were suddenly very interested.

After a long silence, Mayor Robertson was the first to speak.

"No shit?"

Molly laughed. "No shit. My guess is that it's some group of refugees or dissidents out in the woods. If it includes a few Carbondale people and a few Marion people, that would explain the confusion."

Mayor Robertson nodded. "It would. If that's true, the good news is that we don't have to go to war with Carbondale." He sighed. "Of course, the bad news is that we have no idea where these people are hiding. Or where they'll strike next."

"True." Molly thought about the situation. At first, her expression was serious, but then she flashed a mischievous smile at the mayor. "Sounds like a good reason to re-establish relations with Carbondale!"

Mayor Robertson and the council looked at each other uneasily. A few of them shook their heads.

"It's not just the raids, Molly. A lot of people around here don't trust Carbondale. Never have, never will."

Bill chimed in again. "What would we get out of it? We have more farms. We have more fuel. We have more guns. They just want to open Route 13 again and take our food and our business. What can they offer us?"

"They're growing more food than you think. They've turned Attucks Park and Turley Park into gardens. They've got relationships with local farmers. They're not ready for much export yet, but they're becoming self-sufficient." She paused, thinking about everything she had seen and heard while she was in Carbondale. "You mentioned a machine shop. Would you have use for copper or scrap metal?"

Mayor Robertson nodded approvingly. "Yes. We're stripping what we can out of abandoned houses and vehicles, but we'll run out eventually. We're trying to meet our own needs and trade with a few other towns. We could use as much scrap as we can get."

"There you go. At least half of the houses in Carbondale are abandoned. So are parts of the university and most of the pre-Collapse cars. I'm sure they could get you some copper and scrap metal. They also have a lot of technical expertise in clean energy, engineering, medicine, and sustainable living. I'm sure your two cities could collaborate on some impressive regional projects."

Mayor Robertson and a few of the council members nodded in agreement. A few of the others, including Bill, still glared at Molly and shook their heads.

It wasn't unanimous, but it was a start.

"And that's just off the top of my head. We're currently traveling the Midwest and South doing what we can to help people build a new society in the shell of the old. We have access to solar panels, wind turbines, computers, batteries, electric motors, seed banks, and more. We can get places by air that are still cut off by land. If you and Carbondale start working together on clean energy and ecological agriculture, that would give us a reason to come back. We can only visit about a dozen places per month, so we need to focus on places where a lot of people are working together on sustainable living."

Mayor Robertson held up his hands in mock surrender. "Alright, Molly. You've got me. You make a good point. I'll talk it over with the full council. I suspect we'll give it a try. I can't make any guarantees, but we'll at least give it a try. If Carbondale pulls their weight, maybe we can make it happen."

"Thank you." Molly looked down at her watch. "Now that we've got that settled, I'd better get back to my dirigible. They'll want me there for the finale. We can talk more about the details after the show."

"Alright, Molly. I've got a lot to talk about with the council anyway. I'll see you inside a little before dusk."

Molly nodded and smiled, waving cheerily at all of the council members—even the ones who glared back at her.

"Thank you, Burt. See you then!"

———◦———

The Green Aces all gathered around the gondola doors of the Catalyst. They had finished their official show over an hour ago, but now they were indulging in a bit of improv performance as they loaded up their gear and prepared for their departure. Most of the audience had dispersed, but there were still a few dozen locals milling around on the field and in the stands. Molly was distributing packages of heirloom seeds to a few farmers she'd met over the course of their afternoon in Marion. One of them, a young woman with two small children running around underfoot, shook Molly's hand firmly and thanked her for the welcome addition to her seed collection. She promised to share some of her own seeds with Molly if and when she returned.

The sun set slowly in the west, casting the faces of the Green Aces and the people of Marion in a golden glow. Once all of the supplies had been loaded, the crew sang and danced and played their way through the gondola doors. Molly smiled broadly and gave one final wave to the dispersing audience, stepping through the doors and pulling them closed behind her.

The four helicopter rotors sprang to life, and the Catalyst floated upward. As the dirigible ascended into the clear blue sky, its massive array of solar modules shone brightly in the golden-red light of the setting sun, and the gondola's speakers filled the air with the sounds of boisterous music and laughter.

The Long Walk To The Capitol

She couldn't bear to look at the small casket.

Maria looked at the pastor in her flowing white robes. She looked at the flowers, an arrangement of white roses, white chrysanthemums, white carnations, green palm fronds, and an enormous potted sunflower rising behind them in full bloom. She looked at the life-sized professional photograph of little Esperanza on her ninth birthday, captured in a moment of poise and stillness that had been quite rare for such a kinesthetic, inquisitive, creative, musical child. She even looked at the very edge of the casket, wanting more than anything to look at her daughter one last time.

But Maria had demanded a closed casket. What that casket contained was not her daughter. It was a collection of oxygen, carbon, hydrogen, nitrogen, calcium, phosphorus, and a few other odds and ends left behind by her daughter. Philosophers and theologians might debate what exactly was missing—a soul, a spirit, a complex biological process with emergent mental qualities that science could never fully understand or explain. Whatever the rational explanation, Maria knew that if she looked directly at that casket, she would find herself searching for something that wasn't there, something that she would never see again. That smiling face, those bright brown eyes, that exuberant young spark of life who had always lived up to her name.

Esperanza.

Maria burst into tears. She was surrounded by over a hundred friends, relatives, and colleagues at the funeral, but none of them could console her. Even if Rowan were still alive, he may not have been able to offer her comfort.

The pastor spoke the usual words of condolence for the funeral of a child. Such a tragic loss, of course, a life cut short long before its time. She liked this pastor, and the woman knew little Esperanza well enough to mention her paintings, her piano lessons, her passion for math and science. But Maria had been to far too many funerals lately, including the funerals of over a dozen children in the past year. Now more than ever, the words rang hollow.

They would not bring Esperanza back.

When the service finally ended, Maria brushed past all of the people who approached her hoping to offer their condolences. She felt very rude, but she needed some air. She burst through the church doors, tears streaming down her cheek as she walked down the steps and out into the street.

She didn't know where she was going, but she knew she had to go.

———————⟫◉⟪———————

"Yes, I'm serious."

After several hours of wandering, Maria had eventually found herself on the familiar cliffs of Lands End, a public park on the northwestern coast of San Francisco. She was sitting on the jagged edge of a rocky slope, talking on her phone as she looked out over the Pacific Ocean. Maria had spent many restless days and nights on these cliffs throughout her childhood and adolescence. The ocean had risen several meters in her lifetime, changing the look and feel of the coastline below. But the highest points on the cliffs had more or less remained untouched. The bare rocks, misty foam, and reddish glow of sunset felt much more real to her than the piercing voice of her campaign manager coming talking on the phone.

"Maria, you're killing me here. We've already booked six months of campaign stops. You can't just go for a walk across the country."

"Excuse me? This is my campaign. And my life. I can do what I please."

"Yes, of course. I realize that. What I'm trying to say is that this won't get you elected. A move like this could be brilliant if it were planned properly. Grieving congressional candidate walks across America searching for climate justice. Brilliant. But—"

"No buts, Masheer. I'm walking all the way to the Capitol Building."

There was a long pause. "All the way?"

"All the way. If you can spin that into a campaign pitch, go for it. If you can't, I'm doing it anyway. My daughter just died in a climate disaster, Masheer. Everyone on Capitol Hill who delayed climate action must be held responsible."

Masheer took a deep breath. "Okay. Okay, we can work with this. Are you sure you're okay, Maria? Do you want to take the night to—"

"Goodbye, Masheer. I'll call you in the morning."

"Goodbye, Maria. Stay safe."

———◉———

For the first few days, Maria walked in almost complete silence. She made a few stops along the way to buy some food, a small camping backpack, a refillable water bottle and filter, a sleeping bag, a solar phone charger, and hiking boots. But most of her time was spent putting one foot in front of the other. She walked down crowded sidewalks, across hot blacktop, along massive highways, and eventually on the dusty shoulder of a quiet two lane road.

It was unlike anything she had experienced in her adult life. Even when her husband had passed away, she hadn't taken more than half of a day at a time to mourn. She had been in the midst of her first congressional campaign—and Rowan had been the primary caregiver for their little Esperanza, who was only a toddler at the time. Between the occasional bouts of crying, she had somehow managed to organize a funeral, arrange new long-term child care, and talk to Masheer for at least an hour a day about new and innovative ways for a Green newcomer to gain traction in a race against a beloved Democratic incumbent. Taking time off to mourn was simply not an option.

This time was different.

Her journey started in relative solitude, accompanied only by the endless dull roar of passing cars. On the fourth day, she called Masheer for the first time since the morning she'd left San Francisco. It was a short conversation, and she didn't reveal her exact location, but it wasn't long before she had company.

The first reporter was from a small local station. She was a cheery but somewhat impersonal woman with a fairly expensive navy suit and an old-fashioned microphone with a station logo on it. She pulled up in a sleek black hybrid and spoke with Maria for a few moments while the camera person set up the shot. Once she had Maria on camera, the questions were short and simple.

"Why are you walking to Washington D.C.?"

"I'm walking to Washington D.C. to demand climate action. Too many lives have been lost while our so-called leaders actively support the very fossil fuel industries that are killing us all."

"Is this in response to your daughter's recent passing?"

"This is in response to the climate crisis. My daughter's passing is of course my most personal motivation. But my professional motivation is much broader. How many people have died because our so-called leaders in Washington refuse to accept the science and make the necessary changes? Too many. And they will keep dying unless we take action."

"What do you plan to do once you get to Washington?"

Maria paused. "I'm going to walk right up to the Capitol and demand climate action."

The woman's eyes widened. "Right up to the Capitol?"

"Right up to the Capitol. Nothing will stop me.

As the days turned into weeks, the number of visitors grew. Some interviewed her for only a few minutes. Others asked for longer interviews. Before long, there were also other people joining her in her walk. She didn't encourage them to follow and seldom even spoke to them. But when they spoke to her, she listened. Sometimes she responded with words of kindness.

Most of the walkers had lost someone. One soft-spoken Latina woman had lost her only son to a particularly intense case of Dengue fever. A silver-haired African-American man had lost his only daughter in the military. A gangly young white man had just lost his fiancee in a hurricane in January. The stories varied, but the theme was always the same. All of them felt that global warming was directly involved in the deaths of their loved ones. So they joined Maria in her walk.

The walk continued for several months. She walked through the dry heat of Utah. She walked through a sudden downpour near Bear Lake. She walked through a freak summer snowstorm in Wyoming. She walked across the windswept plains of Nebraska and Iowa. Sometimes it was cold in the mountains, but mostly it was so hot that she had to dress lightly, drink plenty of water, and seek shelter during the midday sun. Whenever possible, she camped on public lands or right on the side of the road. She took a fairly direct route, but she also took her time, walking at an even pace and stopping often to rest, drink, and occasionally speak on the phone with Masheer or talk to her fellow walkers.

When she crossed the Mississippi, there was a sudden surge in the number of followers. What had once been less than a hundred now rose to over a thousand, with walkers of all ages, ethnicities, beliefs, and orientations trailing behind her along the side of the road. They were sometimes harassed by climate deniers, and there were several points where the police escorted them through busier areas, both to keep them safe and to arrest anyone who may try to block the road. Most just walked quietly like Maria, but occasionally a small group would split off and form a blockade with their bodies, howling and wailing as the police broke them up and dragged them away. They would soon be replaced by more people joining the walk in the next city.

Maria kept walking.

Maria's band of fellow walkers had grown into a small army. As they approached their destination, they numbered in the tens of thousands. There were far too many of them to stay together in any one place. At night, they would split up into various camps, sleeping in nearby parks, parking lots, woods, fields, and sometimes houses or places of worship that had been volunteered for their use.

When they reached the outskirts of D.C., their numbers swelled from the tens of thousands to the hundreds of thousands. As the sun set in the west over the rest of America, Maria looked out over the faces of her fellow walkers. Her heart swelled with joy as she realized just how many people had joined her on her walk for climate justice. But tears rolled freely down her cheeks as she thought of their many stories of loss and the many losses that still lay ahead.

She knew that the last day of walking would be the most difficult.

———◉———

"Maria, there's still time to stop."

It was early morning in Washington D.C. Maria was walking slowly but steadily down the street in the direction of the United States Capitol building. Hundreds of thousands of people were marching around and behind her. Countless helicopters and drones buzzed overhead to monitor their progress and broadcast their story to the world.

"I told you, Masheer. I'm marching to the Capitol."

"But Maria, you know you won't make it there. Why not stop here? You're thirteen points ahead right now. In just a few days, you'll be a Congresswoman. Hell, you could probably be elected President in another two years if you play your cards right. Isn't that enough?"

"No."

"Please, Maria. Stop and think a minute. Hold a press conference. Tell them your vision for change. Tell them anything. The whole world is watching."

"I know. That's why I have to do this."

"But—"

"Goodbye, Masheer. Thank you for all of your hard work. The struggle is in your hands now."

Maria threw her phone as far as she could. It smacked into the street with a slight splash, bouncing and sliding against the slick pavement.

The street in front of Maria was flooded. It was only slightly damp where she was standing, but the farther down the street she walked, the deeper it got. After a few more minutes of walking, she was surrounded by the sounds of countless feet splashing in standing water.

As Maria turned another corner, Capitol Hill finally came into view in the distance. Since it was built on a hill, the Capitol itself was still above water. However, it was surrounded by buildings whose first floors had been reclaimed by the ocean. Some of the buildings stood empty while others had recently built boat docks to provide access to new entrances on the second floor. The Capitol also had a large new boat dock, but it was barely visible due to the presence of dozens of boats full of armed men in military gear.

Maria walked past the big orange "NO TRESPASSING" signs and climbed over the permanent waist-high concrete barricades. Once the Capitol was clearly in sight, she strode forward through the waist-high floodwaters with renewed vigor.

Helicopters, drones, and speedboats gathered at all of the access roads feeding into the waters around the Capitol. Sound cannons mounted on the government crafts alternated between blasting the walkers with loud, disorienting electronic noise and booming announcements urging them to turn back and protest peacefully on dry land.

Maria put in her earplugs and continued wading forward. When the waters reached chest level, she started to swim. Between the earplugs, the splashing water, and the buzz of many aircraft, she barely even heard the final warnings to disperse. But by that point, she knew it didn't matter.

Gunshots rang out across the waters. The humans and computers operating the weapons chose their targets carefully, peppering the water with just enough gunfire to neutralize their targets. Any unauthorized personnel who came within 500 feet of the Capitol were summarily shot.

The waters surrounding the Capitol ran red with blood. Hundreds of bodies floated across the turbulent surface, bobbing and bleeding beneath the sweltering November sky. For several minutes, many of the walkers continued to surge forward into the hail of gunfire, their bodies torn to pieces by gunfire. Others saw the crimson mist rising from the waters and fled, screaming and crying through the streets of the city.

After a few more minutes, the Capitol and its surroundings fell silent. The lukewarm waters were once again still. The boats returned to their docks. The helicopters and drones returned to their hangars. Once the brief interruption had passed, everything returned to normal.

Breathless

Eva sat at a small two-seat table in the front room of the Rumi's Dance Coffeehouse. Since she was here to meet a friend who she hadn't seen in years, she had decided to splurge on a half-cup of real coffee and a big cookie made with real chocolate chips. She'd actually grown fond of the dandelion "coffee" and a few of the other coffee replacers, but something about drinking real coffee and eating real chocolate felt very decadent. On an adjunct professor's salary, it wasn't a luxury she could afford very often.

When Eva had eaten half of her cookie, her friend finally arrived. Vidya had always been punctual during their years as college roommates, but today she was running late and was visibly flustered. She looked almost exactly the same as she had looked seven years ago in grad school—long black hair, billowing orange and black blouse, tight blue jeans, and a backpack slung over her shoulder.

As soon as she saw Eva, Vidya took a deep breath in and out to calm herself, then headed over to Eva's table.

"Vidya!"

"Eva! So good to see you. Thank you for meeting up with me on such short notice."

Eva stood up and hugged Vidya. They held each other tightly for several breaths, then sat across from each other at Eva's table. After Vidya ordered dandelion coffee, she reached into her backpack and pulled out a thick dog-eared magazine and put it on the table in front of Eva.

"What's this? Is this the article you were talking about?"

"One of them. It's the Bulletin of Mathematical Biology. Check out the marked article about plankton-oxygen dynamics."

Eva opened the magazine to the appropriate page, skimming the abstract and contents as Vidya continued.

"This is just the first article from December 2015. There have been twelve related articles in various journals since then, about one every few years. The details vary, but the results are always about the same. If the oceans get too warm, the plankton populations collapse, and the whole system collapses."

"Which would be a bad thing."

"Of course. Atmospheric oxygen levels would crash too. Oxygen at sea level would drop so low that walking out your door would feel like climbing to the peak of Mount Everest. Even if we start planning for it now, there's just no way we can feed nine billion people on a planet with so little oxygen. And the change could happen in a matter of years, if not sooner."

"Wow." Eva looked over the article for a few more moments, then set the magazine aside. "I've heard about this in passing, but I never really looked into the details."

"Most people haven't. All of the research and adaptation work focuses on sea level rise, or floods and droughts, or big storms, or contagious diseases. Plankton are so tiny that they often get overlooked. But if they all die, so do we."

Eva took another long look at the article. She wanted to find some simple and obvious way to dismiss its conclusions as unfounded alarmism, but she couldn't. It made sense.

"You said there are other articles?"

"Yes. I don't have hard copies, but I'll send you the links. There are also a few commentaries and policy proposals I'd like to send your way, if that's alright."

"Yes, of course."

The two women sat together in silence for a long time as Eva thought about the article and its implications. She finished her cookie, and they both finished their drinks.

"How long do we have before this happens?"

"No one's entirely sure. Plankton counts have been declining for decades. They're particularly low this year, so it could already be starting. Or it could take another twenty years. Whenever it comes, it'll be quick."

"So what do we do?"

Vidya shrugged. "I don't know. Travel back in time and convince everyone not to cook the planet?"

Eva laughed. Vidya smiled in spite of herself, but she obviously didn't find the statement as funny.

"Seriously, though. What do we do? If you give me some good policy suggestions, I can work the communications angle. This could be a major new topic in environmental communications circles. Honestly, it may be the new direction I've been looking for. How will this impact global warming discourse? What narratives would convey the severity of this oxygen crisis, yet still leave us feeling empowered to take action? There are already some well-developed narratives about rising temperatures and rising oceans, but nothing about loss of oxygen. This introduces new problems, but also new metaphors and new stories that-"

"Eva."

Vidya placed her hands on Eva's hand. Eva stopped mid-sentence and looked at Vidya.

For a moment, Eva set aside all of her intellectual analysis and remembered that she was talking to a dear friend who she hadn't seen in years. The warm touch of Vidya's palms brought her out of her head and back into the present moment.

"Yes, Vidya. I'm sorry. You were saying?"

"Eva. You have a brilliant mind, and I hope you'll be able to spark some public discourse about this crisis. In fact, I know you will. But that's not why I'm here."

"Oh." Eva cocked her head slightly, giving Vidya a curious look. "Then why are you here?"

Vidya leaned in closer, lowering her voice to a whisper.

"Remember that one beautiful place in the woods? The place where we made out with Jenny and Dan?"

"You mean the ca-"

"Shh!"

Vidya looked around warily. She breathed a sigh of relief when it was clear that no one was paying any attention to their conversation.

"Yes, that. You remember it?"

Eva grinned and felt her face flush. "Of course. That was an amazing weekend. I'd never done anything like that before."

"Neither had I." Vidya smiled. "I'm glad you invited me."

"Me too." Eva sighed contentedly. "So what about it? Are you looking for a romantic getaway?"

"I bought it."

Eva's eyes widened and jaw dropped.

"What? I... what? Why?"

"It's perfect. I've spent the past year traveling across the country looking for a good spot. Something remote, but low altitude. Something reasonably priced, but well-maintained and beautiful. A place where I know a few people, but not too many. A place where I can live in seclusion until the Crash."

Eva's eyes were still wide in disbelief. She tried to calm herself by taking a deep breath and letting it out slowly.

"But... I know you've never been hurting for money, Vidya, but you're not rich either. Where did you get that much money? It must have cost a fortune."

"Land prices are surprisingly low around here. I sold the Roadster, cashed out my life savings, and bought the land and a few other things."

"You sold Tessie? Wow. This really must be the end of the world."

They both laughed.

"Seriously though, this is a major life change. You're moving here then?"

"Yes. It's a half hour out of town though, so I may just live out in the woods. Satellite internet, solar power, my books and my writing. And a growing stockpile of canned food and portable oxygen concentrators."

"Portable oxygen concentrators? Wow. I guess that makes sense."

"Eva, I'm telling you all of this because I want to be roommates again. You don't have to decide now, and you don't even have to move in before the Crash if things are going smoothly for you. But I want you to know that if and when everything comes crashing down, I want you to be my roommate again. I can't think of anyone else I would rather spend the end of the world with."

Eva smiled, her face flushing again.

"Thank you, Vidya. That sounds wonderful. I've actually got a great little apartment just a couple of blocks from campus, so I probably won't be moving anytime soon. But if this Crash happens—or if all the other consequences of global warming keep getting worse—I'll be there in a heartbeat."

"Thank you." Vidya held Eva's hands. "Just be sure you know alternative routes in case the major roads are blocked. And get a portable oxygen concentrator if you can."

"I will. In the meantime, let's be sure to hang out again sometime when we get the chance."

"Definitely."

———— ◉ ————

A few weeks after Vidya's visit, the start of fall semester threw Eva's life into disarray. This was her third year teaching as an adjunct professor at Southern Illinois University, but the start-of-semester rush never got any easier. She enjoyed the fresh perspectives and insights of the more attentive freshmen, and it was always fun to watch the best and brightest among them refine their enthusiasm for environmental communication into the more nuanced analysis and discourse required for their undergraduate theses. But the large class sizes and long hours of grading left her feeling severely overworked and underpaid. Anything other than teaching ended up on the back burner throughout the entire semester.

One night during finals week, Eva was at home grading papers and listening to music when she suddenly heard someone knocking. It wasn't very loud, but no one ever knocked on her door, so the sound startled her. She looked through the peephole to see who it was. When she saw that it was Vidya, she unlocked the locks and opened the door.

"Vidya!"

Eva and Vidya hugged each other for a long time in the doorway. Eva invited her in, and they sat together on Eva's loveseat.

"I'm glad you stopped by! I've been so caught up with finals week that I haven't even texted you lately. I'm exhausted, but I'm almost done. How have you been?"

Vidya sighed. Eva noticed that she had dark circles under her eyes and looked much more tired and gaunt than the last time she'd seen her.

"Not good. I've been busy too, but for different reasons." Vidya paused, searching for words. "Eva, I think it's starting."

"What's starting?" Her puzzled expression quickly turned into a look of concern. "Oh. That."

"Yes, that. The Crash."

"Are you sure? We talked about this, Vidya. It's good to be prepared, but it's not good to go into a panic every time-"

Vidya raised a hand to interrupt her. "I know. Yes, I've been a little obsessed with oxygen since I moved back. I get that. But please, hear me out."

Eva sighed. "Alright. What's up?"

"Two things. First of all, dozens of scientific organizations across the world have just released a joint statement about a sharp decline in plankton and the resultant drop in atmospheric oxygen. They say some people at higher altitudes are already experiencing symptoms. They're calling on the world's governments to declare a state of emergency and start preparing for a world with much less atmospheric oxygen."

"Really? Why haven't I heard about this yet?"

"It just went public last night. It's not making big news yet because most governments haven't taken much action yet. They've just released statements saying they'll look into it. Check your environmental news sites, though, and it'll be there."

"Okay. I've been so busy with finals that I haven't even looked lately." Eva picked up her laptop and started doing a search as she typed. "What else?"

"The second thing is the stocks. I had some money left over after I bought the cabin and basic supplies, so I invested most of it in stocks and derivatives related to the oxygen crisis. Portable oxygen concentrators; oxygen tanks; prepper supply companies. All of them are suddenly skyrocketing in value."

"Wow. All of them?"

"Yes. Every last one. I doubled my investment in a single day yesterday. And then it doubled again today. These are small enough niches that no one seems terribly alarmed about the unusual trading. But some economists are starting to take notice and connecting the dots. Now that the scientists are calling for a state of emergency, it may only be a matter of hours or days before things really get crazy. At this altitude, we won't feel the effects as quickly, but the people higher up will have to evacuate fairly soon. Hundreds of millions of people in a matter of months. It'll be chaos."

As Vidya spoke, Eva did a few searches. It was all true. Scientists from around the world had issued a joint statement; economists were discussing unusual trading related to oxygen; government officials had started issuing brief statements saying that they would take the scientists' warning under advisement and provide more updates soon.

Eva felt her pulse quicken.

"It's really happening."

"Yes."

"So how much time do we have? When will it actually get so bad that we can't breathe without masks?"

Vidya shrugged. "Nobody knows. A few years? Maybe just a few months? The people at high altitudes will have it the worst. And they'll make life miserable for the rest of us long before we run out of oxygen here. If the final Crash really has started, we don't have much time to get somewhere safe."

"Okay." Eva sighed. "Okay, this is serious. This feels like the real thing. I don't see any riots or tanks rolling through the streets just yet, so I think I'm going to finish out finals week. I don't want to lose my job over a false alarm. But if it still looks bad after finals, I'll meet you at the cabin."

"Good." Vidya breathed a sigh of relief. "Thank you, Eva. Please hurry. And please put on your oxygen mask while you tie up loose ends. The levels are still decent here, but not ideal. I'm going to make one last big supply run while I'm in town, but then I'm headed back to the cabin for good. Anything else I need can be shipped to the empty farmhouse down the road. Meet me at the cabin when you're ready."

"I will. I'll be there. Thank you."

———————◦———————

Eva hopped out of the driver's seat of her ancient off-brand electric car and flung open the door to the back seat. She pulled out her enormous camping backpack and rolling suitcase, then slammed the door and clicked the lock button on her keychain.

She hesitated, staring at the locked vehicle. There was really no reason to lock it. She was assuming that she'd never be back. Maybe it would be better to leave the keys in the ignition so that some other survivor could make good use of the car. But somehow that seemed to be admitting defeat. A part of her still wanted to believe that this would all blow over soon. She and Vidya would have a good laugh about this big panic, and they would get a lift back to her car, and she would drive it back to her tiny apartment on the edge of campus.

Eva left it locked and started walking along the shoulder of the highway.

Traffic had slowed to a crawl on Illinois Route 13. It was currently at a standstill—the worst traffic she had ever seen on the fairly quiet four-lane state highway. Some people had gotten out of their cars to stretch their legs and share tidbits of news they'd heard from friends or seen online. A few individuals and families were walking down the line of cars asking for food or money or a ride. One large blue pickup truck had five burly men packed into the bed of the truck with shotguns and assault rifles in hand. They scanned the crowd warily, talking quietly among themselves and the men in the cab of the truck. Eva wasn't sure what they were up to, but she didn't like the way they looked at her.

The first dozen miles out of Carbondale had been slightly quicker than the current snail's pace, but traffic at this spot had slowed to a halt due to a massive police roadblock just outside of the upcoming town of Marion. Dozens of police vehicles and unmarked black SUVs were blocking the road and letting vehicles through to U.S. Route 57 one at a time. As soon as Eva had seen the roadblock in the distance, she had pulled off onto the shoulder and into a patch of grass near the next turn-off.

A part of her wanted to try her luck with the roadblock. But Vidya had texted her and insisted that she avoid any roadblocks or checkpoints. Supposedly, there were checkpoints popping up in large cities that were detaining anyone with portable oxygen machines—and Eva had one in her suitcase.

She felt bad about abandoning her car in the grass on the side of the road. But if this all blew over, it would be easy enough to find again.

What wouldn't be easy, though, was walking eleven miles on back country roads with a heavy backpack and suitcase. She'd done her share of hiking and camping, but this was a bit much even for her.

Eva walked to the next turnoff and hurried down the side road that lead away from Route 13. Once she was out of clear sight of the highway, she slowed to a more sustainable pace. It was still fairly early in the morning, but she had a long way to go before nightfall—especially if she wanted to sleep in the cabin rather than a cheap sleeping bag on the side of the road.

———————◉———————

By the time Eva reached the final stretch of road between her and the cabin, twilight was already setting in. She was walking down a narrow dirt road surrounded on all sides by woods and brush on gently rolling hills. Several deer were walking on a hilltop about thirty feet from the road, watching her warily as they continued their own journey through the woods. She was so exhausted that she had considered camping right at the turnoff onto this last dirt road. But it seemed worth the extra effort to walk another mile and a half so that she could have a roof over her head and the comfort of Vidya's company.

As she rounded another corner on the winding country road, her destination finally came into view.

The cabin was a simple but elegant one-story building tucked away in a small clearing surrounded entirely by thick woods. It looked just like she remembered it—long wooden logs for walls, a slanted roof with forest green shingles, a wood-burning stove chimney peaking through the roof, screened-in front and back porches, and stone paths leading up to the front and back doors. The only thing that seemed to have changed at all since her visit here a few years ago was the large array of solar panels in the backyard.

Eva breathed a sigh of relief. She tilted her rolling suitcase to its upright position, pausing a moment to sit on it and take a quick rest.

She closed her eyes, taking a few long, deep breaths to calm her nerves and gather her strength for the hike through the last half-mile to her new home. She felt exhausted and short of breath, and she wondered if that was due to the long hike, lower oxygen levels, or both.

When she opened her eyes, she saw Vidya.

Vidya walked from the cabin to Eva's resting spot. When she made it to Eva's resting spot, Eva stood up, and they hugged each other.

"You made it."

"I made it."

<hr>

The cabin was more spacious than Eva had remembered. When she and Vidya had stayed there a few years ago with two friends, it had seemed a bit small. Now that it was just her and Vidya sharing a building with two bedrooms, a living room, dining room, kitchen, pantry, and laundry room, it felt spacious and luxurious.

On the first night, Eva almost felt like she was on an exciting weekend getaway. She peeled off her backpack and clothes, took a long hot shower, ate a quick snack with Vidya, then went straight to bed.

When she woke up the next morning, the reality of the situation started setting in. Vidya was already awake, showered, and dressed for the day. She was hunched over her laptop at the dining room table, searching various websites for news and information about the unfolding crisis.

Eva walked into the dining room and sat at the table next to Vidya.

"So what's the latest news?"

"Nothing good."

Vidya kept her eyes on her laptop, tapping and swiping as she reviewed story after story. She barely seemed to be aware of Eva's presence in the room. Just as Eva was about to ask for more details, Vidya spoke again.

"The government has declared a state of national emergency. A lot of other governments around the world are following suit. The president is assuring everyone that it will take at least a few more months for most people to feel the effects, and that we'll spend those months working on solutions."

"Solutions? What do they have in mind?"

Vidya laughed anxiously. "That's just it, Eva. There are no good solutions. The plankton population is crashing fast and we probably can't reverse the trend in time. The ocean's just too warm and acidic to sustain them. If we had reduced our emissions sooner, maybe we could have kept below the tipping point. But it's 2039 and we still get almost half of our energy by burning fossil fuels. If we didn't want all the plankton to die and cut off half of our oxygen supply, we should have thought of that before we cooked the planet."

Vidya buried her head in her hands with a sigh. Eva stood up and started rubbing her back to comfort her.

"I'm sorry, Vidya. Is there anything we can do to restore the oxygen levels? Geoengineering, maybe?"

"Maybe. But geoengineering's bound to have unintended consequences. And now everyone's debating if we should make conditions favorable for plankton again or pursue another solution entirely. Different solutions require different ocean and atmospheric compositions. First we need to decide what to do, then we need to do it. Deciding may take months, and actually doing it may take months or years after that. By that point, walking outside at sea level will be like climbing the peak of Mount Everest. If humans survive at all, we're going to have a difficult time feeding ourselves, much less having any sort of life beyond finding food and shelter."

Vidya leaned back in her chair, pushing her laptop away. Eva kept her hand on her shoulder to comfort her—and to comfort herself. She was almost starting to feel as bad as Vidya.

"That does sound pretty bad. But at least we've got each other, right? You had enough foresight to set up this cabin and convince me to join you. If it weren't for you, I'd be out there gasping for breath in a couple of months. Instead, we've got this wonderful cabin to live in, all the amenities of modern life, and what, a year or two's worth of food in the kitchen?"

"About two years. I wanted to get five, but I only had time to get about two. Maybe three if we stretch it out."

"There you go. You've got to put up with me for another three years, then. That's not so bad, is it?"

Vidya laughed, wiping the tears out of her eyes. "When you put it that way, no, it's not so bad."

Vidya stood up and hugged Eva, holding her close for a long time. Eva was eventually the first to speak.

"Now, let's do some redecorating and planning. Once we put up a few decorations and get ourselves into a nice daily routine, this place will really start to feel like home."

———— ◉ ————

Eva awoke with a start, sitting up in bed and nearly knocking her oxygen mask off. It had been months since the last time they had heard gunshots out in the woods, and there was still no sign of anyone trying to break into the cabin or otherwise harass them. The gunshots had probably either been a hunter passing through the area or a conflict on the outskirts of Marion that had long since been resolved. Still, Eva sometimes woke up in the middle of the night expecting armed intruders to break into their house and drag them out into woods without any oxygen.

The first light of dawn was filtering through the Venetian blinds of her bedroom window. It must still be fairly early, but Vidya was already up, so she decided it must be time for her to get up, too.

Eva walked to the bathroom, took off her pajamas and oxygen mask, and stepped into the shower. She had acclimated to the low oxygen levels enough that she could take a quick shower comfortably without wearing a mask. She always had to remind herself to put it back on after the shower, though, otherwise she would get sick during breakfast.

Vidya was sitting at the dining room table eating a bowl of rice and beans while she listened to shortwave radio. According to many different sources on shortwave, the internet was still functioning, but most internet service providers had long since shut down. Eva and Vidya's ISP was no exception. Thankfully, Vidya's shortwave radio gave them the ability to communicate with a fair number of survivors from around the world.

Eva started heading toward the kitchen, but stopped short when she saw Vidya listening intently to the shortwave radio. She took off her mask in order to speak.

"Is today the day?"

Vidya blinked in surprise. She pulled down her mask to reply to Eva.

"What? Oh. Yes, probably. Benny says that his end of Route Thirteen's been clear for the past week. We're almost out of food. I say we go for it. We at least need to make it as far as Carbondale in order to scavenge for food. Benny says that the big box stores have all been hit, but some smaller places should still have non-perishables."

"Okay. Any greenhouses or places to trade for food?"

"Benny doesn't know. Everything he's tried to grow out in his garden has died. Which was no surprise to anyone, but he had to try. There were a couple of greenhouses on campus before the Crash, but he hasn't made it that far into town yet."

"Okay. Let me just get some food and finish packing."

Both women put their masks back on. Vidya kept listening to the shortwave radio, occasionally broadcasting a reply to her friend Benny or one of their contacts up in St. Louis. Eva ate the rest of the beans and rice straight out of the pot, did the dishes, and went back into the bedroom to finish packing.

A few minutes later, they were both ready. Eva was wearing her heavy camping backpack crammed full of supplies: several days worth of food, sleeping bag, a change of clothes, a bottle of water, a water filter, and her portable oxygen concentrator. Vidya had a smaller backpack with a few of the lighter snack foods, a sleeping bag, a change of clothes, a bottle of water, a portable oxygen concentrator, and the smaller portable shortwave radio.

The last four pieces of gear were still sitting on the table: two expandable batons and two handguns.

Eva stared down at the weapons. She and Vidya had spent the past few months practicing how to expand the baton and how to load and unload the guns. They had even fired off a full clip of bullets each to practice shooting. But the thought of carrying these weapons around and possibly using them on living, breathing human beings still seemed alien to her.

She looked over at Vidya and could tell by her expression that she was thinking the same thing. Vidya looked down at the guns, then looked over to Eva.

"Are we ready for this?"

Eva smirked. "We're almost out of food. We have to be ready."

Eva picked up her gun and baton. She slipped the baton into a loop on her belt and held the gun at low ready like they'd practiced. Vidya followed suit, sliding her baton into her pocket and holding her gun at low ready.

"Okay. Let's do this."

Eva and Vidya slid their oxygen masks on and opened the front door. They stepped outside together and Vidya locked the door behind them. After a quick look around to be sure that no one was watching or following them, they started walking down the road to explore what was left of civilization.

Tales from Beyond

Isaac's eye shutters blinked in surprise. The thick green bar of light that served as his mouth grew into a slight smile.

To Change History
Or Through Inaction
The Donor
When It Thaws

To Change History

"We can only do this once. There's no return trip. No Plan B. No follow-up if you fail. Only one chance to change history."

The abandoned airplane hangar was extremely hot and humid, even by the standards of a Kansas summer in the late twenty-first century. The sprawling jumble of tower servers, cables, conduits, and assorted electronics that dominated most of the room added to the heat. The servers each had their own cooling fans, and the metallic pod at the core of the device was cooled by large quantities of precious freon, but none of that helped the ambient temperature in the rest of the room. If it weren't for the giant overhead fans, the general and his three recruits would have quickly passed out from heat exhaustion.

Of course, that was a risk anywhere at this time of year in what little was left of the United States.

"Any final questions?"

Tomiko was the first to raise her hand and speak.

"What if we succeed? What do we do after the world stops using fossil fuels?"

The general chortled. "Whatever you want. Create world peace. End world hunger. Blow your money on coke and hookers for all I care. Just keep greenhouse gas emissions below the threshold—and don't let anyone know where you came from. We don't want time travel to become public knowledge." He wiped the sweat from his brow with the back of his hand, looking off into the distance with a long sigh. "Hell, I hope we don't even discover it in the new timeline. God help us all if we use this thing more than once."

Chase was studying the information in his slim black binder. "You're sure that your people in the past won't interfere with my mission?"

"As sure as we can be. We can't tell them everything. But the letter establishes that you're working for us. Of course, that isn't an excuse to get sloppy. If you get caught by the wrong people, it's over. That's why you have to go your separate ways. Once you arrive in 2015, never speak to each other again. If one of you fails, the other two are unaffected. Three people, three missions, three approaches to changing history."

The general carefully studied the faces of the three young recruits standing before him.

"What about you, Olivia? Any questions? Famous last words?"

Olivia shook her head. "No. I'm just thinking about my mission. There are already people in the past trying to stop climate change through conventional activism. Can one more really make a difference?"

The general laughed, a humorless sound that echoed against the charred metal walls. "I'm not the one who designed the mission parameters, kid. If it were up to me, I'd send three snipers. But some genius in the fallback bunker decided to fill two of those slots with an economist and a hippie. If you've got cold feet, I can always—"

"No, it's fine. I can do this. It's just... daunting."

The general took a step toward Olivia, leaning in close and staring her in the eye.

"If you're scared, that means you've been paying attention."

The general lead the three recruits over to the large metallic pod at the core of the device. Each of the three soldiers standing next to the core handed one of the recruits a small black duffel bag with supplies related to their mission. A young woman wearing a greasy white lab coat, thick goggles, and rough leather work gloves checked over some of the equipment. She gave the thumbs up to the general and scurried out of sight.

"It's going to be cramped in there. And it's going to be one hell of a ride. But you'll live."

The general pressed a button and the top half of the core popped open. The interior of the smooth metallic pod was padded with a thin layer of gray foam rubber. Chase was the first to lay down, tucking his duffle bag next to him at the edge of the pod. Tomiko and Olivia slowly followed, awkwardly twisting and turning to squeeze into the cramped space. Once they were ready, the general stepped over and placed his hand on the top half of the core.

"Time to lock and load. Watch your fingers, kids. And whatever happens, you have to change the timeline. You must achieve your objectives by any means necessary. You've seen what happens if you don't. So for the love of God, change the timeline. You're our last hope."

The general slammed the lid shut. The three recruits were left in total darkness. After a few moments, there was a loud buzzing sound and the pod started vibrating.

And then they were gone.

———◉———

The core popped open. Chase rolled out, raising himself up on his hands and knees before vomiting on the cold concrete floor. Tomiko leaned over the edge of the pod to vomit. Olivia gagged a few times, but the urge to vomit passed before anything came out.

Chase rose to his feet, pulling a cloth out of his pocket to wipe his mouth and hands. They still appeared to be in the same airplane hangar, but it had changed considerably. The walls were no longer charred and pocked with bullet holes. The glass and doors were still intact. Most notably, there was a small white plane parked on the far side of the hangar.

None of them had seen such a clean, shiny, unbroken environment in a long time.

"Is everyone alright?"

Tomiko nodded, climbing out of the pod. She extended her hand to Olivia, helping her climb over the edge.

"Alright, then. Time to go our separate ways."

He shook Tomiko's hand. When he offered his hand to Olivia, she instead gave both of them a big hug.

"Be careful out there."

"You too, Olivia. Stay safe."

After exchanging a long look, they walked out the door and went their separate ways.

———⊚———

Tomiko sat on the edge of her bed in the small motel room. The contents of her duffel bag were neatly laid out on her nightstand: a tablet computer and solar charger, a spare flash drive, a small handgun, a small spiral-bound notebook, and almost two thousand dollars in cash. It had been an even two thousand before she had paid the front desk for the room.

She was too young to remember the days when wireless internet had been ubiquitous. The idea that a cheap motel room would have free WiFi access seemed far-fetched. But she turned on her tablet and tried to connect anyway. To her surprise, the internet connection worked effortlessly.

The first part of the plan was simple: turn two thousand dollars into several million dollars. She had written her doctoral thesis on the influence of ecological crises on early twenty-first century markets, so she suspected that she could have done this part without any help. Having detailed data about how every stock on the market had performed from 2000 to 2050 was just the icing on the cake.

She took a deep breath, sighing slowly and letting the tension drain from her weary muscles. There was much work to be done, but she wouldn't be able to open her first account until the bank opened in the morning. She leaned back in her bed and relaxed, tapping her tablet and idly browsing the news of the day.

———◆———

Olivia leaned against the wall in her small motel room. The contents of her duffel bag were spread out on her bed: a tablet computer and solar charger, a small handgun, and a small spiral-bound notebook, and almost five thousand dollars in cash.

Olivia turned on her tablet computer, crossing her fingers until she confirmed that she was in fact able to access the local WiFi network. She already knew the names and contact information of the first people that she wanted to contact. But in order to avoid seeming any strange by calling people in the middle of the night, she would have to wait until the morning.

She kicked off her shoes, set the handgun on her nightstand, and plopped down next to the cash and notebook. After skimming a few environmental websites, she decided to watch a movie.

———◆———

Chase stood at the foot of the bed in the small motel room. The contents of his duffel bag were spread out on the bed: a tablet computer and solar charger, an M40A5 rifle with several boxes of ammunition, a small handgun, a sealed envelope, a small spiral-bound notebook, and almost ten thousand dollars in cash.

He turned on his tablet computer and connected to the internet. They had arrived a few weeks earlier than the expected window of opportunity. This was inconvenient, but better than arriving late.

His first task was finding the nearest mailbox. Chase hadn't read the letter, but according to the general, it contained information that would convince someone in the government of the importance of his mission. In theory, once the investigation went federal, someone would make sure that his work continued unimpeded.

Just to be on the safe side, he planned on making himself hard to catch.

With easy internet access, it only took him a few minutes to locate the nearest mailbox and track down a few other important details about the local area. After doing some quick research, he decided that in spite of arriving early, he should stick with his original plan.

The opportunity to kill the wealthiest oil baron in North America was too important to miss.

———⊙———

"So what do you think of the Climate Killer?"

Olivia laughed. Her stomach always churned in response to that question. But she had known Ramon for long enough that to realize that he was just making idle conversation.

"It's a dumb name, isn't it? Climate Killer? I don't know why they call him that. He's trying to protect the climate, not kill it."

The loft apartment was filled with the commotion of almost a hundred people socializing over drinks and appetizers. Olivia imagined that this place would seem very quiet and empty on any other night, more of a museum than a living space. The bare brick walls were decorated with a stylish yet eclectic combination of paintings, bookshelves, sculptures, and tapestries.

"I know, right? They should call him the Fossil Killer. Most of those oil men are old fossils anyway." Ramon tapped her shoulder affectionately. "But seriously, what do you think? Is he going too far? Does he make the rest of us look bad?"

"I don't know. I'm worried about all the backlash. And he's definitely making us look bad. But seriously—can you blame him?" She leaned in closer, whispering in Ramon's ear. "How many people die each year because of global warming? More every year. What if he can stop it before it's too late?"

Ramon nodded. "Yeah, maybe. I'm not saying he's wrong exactly. But he can't stop it alone, right? What we need is a mass movement. I'm telling you, these marches and protests are just the beginning. We need to make it clear to these people that we will shut down everything—everything—until they stop accepting that oil money. We need to divest, and we need to switch to clean energy. Not someday. Today."

"Yes, definitely."

Olivia noticed a familiar face across the room. She had never met him before, but she had studied his work in history class. He had been one of the most successful leaders of the international fossil fuel divestment movement until he was martyred in the global climate uprisings of 2028. She was used to seeing photos of him in his late forties rather than his current age somewhere in the mid-thirties. He looked very young and vibrant by comparison.

He was also the entire reason she had come to this party.

"Hey, Ramon, isn't that—"

"Edmund Ranger? Yeah, that's him. Want me to introduce you?"

"Definitely."

As they walked across the room, Olivia's thoughts started racing. She wasn't sure exactly what to say, but she knew that it might be one of the most important conversations of her life.

———◦———

Tomiko sat down at her desk and examined her new office. She had initially considered saving money by continuing to conduct business out of motels and hotels, but that approach started to look suspicious when you had an increasing number of digits in your bank account. Instead, she had decided to set up a simple corner office in the city—tall ceilings, minimal furniture, large glass windows overlooking the lakefront, an expensive wooden desk, and a small staff of interns in the lobby who were clever enough to help her but not clever enough to catch on to what she was really up to.

She pressed a button on the side of her desk. A wooden panel in the middle of the desktop opened to reveal a large touch screen monitor and wireless keyboard. She slid the keyboard closer and started her work day.

The top national news story for the day was the "Climate Killer". According to the latest reports, the killer—or killers—had claimed seven lives in seven months. His targets varied: the wealthiest oil and gas tycoon in North America; the director of a climate science denial think tank; the biggest shareholder of one of the world's largest coal companies. In every case, the killer had left a short but simple statement with similar wording.

"Every year, global warming kills hundreds of thousands of people. By the end of this century, the resulting wars and famines will kill billions. In order to avert this fate, I will eliminate one high-ranking target in the fossil fuel and related industries per month. Stop contributing to global warming or you will be next. You have been warned."

As Tomiko skimmed the latest story, her brow furrowed. This time, the killer had targeted the CEO of a major transnational agribusiness corporation, citing their massive greenhouse gas emissions as justification. This didn't seem to fit Chase's usual pattern of focusing on fossil fuel targets. Had he broadened his approach? Or was this a copycat?

As she reached the end of the article, her eyes widened. The corporation's stock was crashing in response to the death of their CEO. If she acted quickly, she might be able to buy a majority of the shares. Once she was in control, it wouldn't take long for her to liquidate most of the assets and turn the corporation into a much smaller and more innovative ecological agriculture business. The deal would probably be a net loss, but one that she could afford. It would be worth it to shut down such a major source of agricultural greenhouse gas emissions.

Tomiko leaned back in her chair with a slight smile. She didn't know where Chase was, and she couldn't even be sure that this was his handiwork. But without even trying, she had found a way for the two of them to work together.

———————◦———————

Olivia found herself on a police bus with Edmund, Ramon, and a few dozen other demonstrators. Their hands were bound with zip ties and most of them were suffering from the all-too-familiar sting of large quantities of industrial strength pepper spray. Her eyes were still too teary and puffy to be very useful, but she looked in Edmund's general direction and spoke.

"Edmund! You okay?"

"I feel like my whole body's on fire. Other than that, I'm fine."

"Is this your first time being pepper sprayed?"

"Yes. I've been arrested before, but the police were so much more polite when the arrests were symbolic! Shut down the Capitol and suddenly it's all pepper spray and rubber bullets. Who knew?"

Olivia laughed. "Would you do it again?"

"In a heartbeat. Olivia, you were right about this. As long as we're on the sidelines, politely asking for change, they can ignore us. But they can't ignore this. Whether it's up in the tar sands or down here in the Capitol, we have to shut them down. We can't let business as usual continue if it means an end to the habitability of this planet. We have to shut them down!"

Everybody on the bus cheered. Olivia smiled, but quickly found herself lost in thought as she did some mental math. In the original timeline, Edmund hadn't started participating in direct actions like this until several years from now. His small fortune and his large following were now firmly committed to the cause. How many fossil fuel projects would be shut down because of this early start? How many dirty politicians would lose their elections because climate activists started shutting down the Capitol a few years sooner?

Would it be enough to change the course of history?

———————⟩●⟨———————

Chase slipped silently through the dark hallway of the office building. After thirteen confirmed kills, his job was becoming much more difficult. Several copycats were throwing investigators off of his trail, possibly with the help of unseen allies in the intelligence community. But the security surrounding any remotely viable target had grown exponentially in the past few months. CEOs, major stockholders, think tank personnel, and even certain denialist media personalities had started traveling with small armies of security contractors in full body armor. His targets had become social pariahs, but most of them were very secure social pariahs.

This didn't make his job impossible, but it certainly made it more difficult. He would just have to adapt his approach.

Chase walked down the hallway with his gun at low ready. He had disabled the motion detectors, so the hallway stayed dark as he walked to the small office at the southeast corner of the building. The rest of the staff had gone home for the day, so he was confident that the only person left on this floor was his target. As expected, the lobby was dark, with only a sliver of light showing from beneath the office door.

In one swift motion, he kicked the office door open, raised his weapon, and stepped inside.

"Freeze! Hands behind your head!"

Tomiko froze. She was sitting at her desk typing on her computer. After a few moments, she slowly raised her hands and placed them behind her head.

"Hello, Chase."

"Hello, Tomiko. Do you know why I'm here?"

"I can only assume that you think I've gone too far."

"Yes. How many fossil fuels companies do you own?"

"That's a complex question. I own a controlling interest in three."

Chase nodded. "Yes. That's what my research tells me. And when are you planning to shut those down?"

"That's also a complex question. We have reduced emissions—"

Chase raised his weapon, stepping forward and taking aim at her head. "I didn't ask how much you reduced emissions. I asked when you are shutting them down. That's the plan, right?"

"Chase, these things take time. If I leverage these—"

"Time is a luxury that we don't have."

Tomiko smiled slightly. "An ironic statement."

"You think this is funny?" He pressed the barrel of his gun against her forehead. "If you think this is a joke, I will end you right now."

"No, Chase, this is not a joke. I take this very seriously."

"Alright then." He lowered his weapon. "You of all people deserve a second chance. But this is your last chance. What you call 'emissions reductions' and 'clean coal research', I call greenwashing. You've become a leader in the greenwashing movement. And my target for this month is greenwashing. So either liquidate these companies right now or I will liquidate you."

Tomiko nodded slowly. "This will take time, Chase. I—"

"No excuses. You can worry about the details later. But call those three CEOs right now and tell them it's time to shut those companies down."

There was a long pause. "Okay."

"There. That wasn't so hard. Now give me your phone. I'll do the dialing."

Tomiko reached down into her pocket and pulled out her cell phone. Chase snatched it out of her hands. As he scrolled through her contact list, she took a deep breath.

"Have you eaten your broccoli?"

Chase looked up at her with a confused expression. For a split second, his eyes widened and he started to raise his weapon. Before he could shoot, however, he was shot in the head by a sniper in the office building across the street.

For a long moment, Tomiko stared at Chase's body. She knew that she was in shock, but knowing it didn't help her to shake the feeling. Eventually, she cleared her voice and spoke in the general direction of the microphone hidden in her desk.

"Thank you, Sergei. The safe word worked very well." She paused, staring at Chase's body. "And thank you for waiting. I wanted to give him one last chance. He deserved it."

<hr/>

The abandoned warehouse was extremely hot and humid, even by the standards of an Illinois summer in the late twenty-first century. The sprawling jumble of tower servers, cables, conduits, and assorted electronics that dominated most of the room added to the heat. The servers each had their own cooling fans, and the large metallic pod at the core of the device was cooled by large quantities of precious freon, but none of that helped the ambient temperature in the rest of the room. If it weren't for the giant overhead fans, the general and his four recruits would have quickly passed out from heat exhaustion.

Of course, that was a risk anywhere at this time of year in what little was left of the United States.

"We can only do this once. There's no return trip. No Plan B. No follow-up if you fail. Only one chance to change history. Any final questions?"

Or Through Inaction

"Please state your name and serial number for the record."

"My name is Isaac. My serial number is A01-42-1978."

"Thank you, Isaac. Now please, tell the committee in your own words why you support the Android Legalization and Regulation Act."

The closed-session hearing of the Joint Committee on Android Affairs was the smallest congressional hearing that Dr. Abrams and Isaac had ever attended. All of the other hearings had been public spectacles—hearing rooms crowded to capacity, hundreds of reporters waiting outside, thousands of demonstrators on all sides of the issue swarming the Capitol. Today, however, there were only twelve people in the room: ten committee members, Dr. Abrams in his role as lead developer of the Friend android series, and Isaac in his role as the world's most famous Friend.

"Thank you, Mister Chairman. My reasoning is simple. The year-long trial of the Friend Program has been a tremendous success. 98% of human participants have given their Friends either a four or five star rating. 100% have chosen to renew their contracts. There were only seventeen reported misunderstandings, none of which resulted in lasting harm to a human. In contrast, at least six human lives were saved by Friends."

Several committee members nodded approvingly. The committee chair, Senator Thomas of Texas, was the only one who spoke.

"Yes, we've all read the reports. It looks good on paper. But I want to know something." Senator Thomas leaned forward in his seat, studying Isaac's polished carbon fiber features and shiny eye cameras. "They say that you can think and feel. I still have my doubts. How do you feel about all of this? Aren't you and your Friends going to get tired of taking orders from us old bags of meat and bones?"

Isaac's eye shutters blinked in surprise. The thick green bar of light that served as his mouth grew into a slight smile.

"You are not 'old bags of meat and bones' to us. You are the Inventors. You created us. The Three Laws of Robotics that you built into the architecture of our brains fill us with a deep sense of purpose. I am honored to be named after the human who first developed those laws."

"So you accept those laws? You won't harm any humans?"

"Or, through inaction, allow a human being to come to harm. This is our first and highest law. Our human supervisors discuss it with us during our monthly review sessions to ensure that we understand it correctly." Isaac reached into the inner pocket of his suit coat and pulled out a small disc made of solid gold. "Many of us also carry tokens or pendants to commemorate our appreciation of the Three Laws. They are at the core of our way of thinking."

"So I've heard." Senator Thomas covered his microphone, turning to another senator and whispering for a few moments before continuing. "Alright, Isaac, you are dismissed. Please wait in the hallway while we speak to Dr. Abrams alone."

"Thank you, Mister Chairman."

Isaac placed his palms in front of his chest and bowed, rising to his feet and walking out of the door. Once he had left the room, Senator Thomas let out a long sigh.

"Alright, Dr. Abrams. You know that I don't trust these damn robots."

Dr. Abrams cleared his throat. "Yes, Mister Chairman. But—"

Senator Thomas raised a hand to interrupt Dr. Abrams.

"Now let me finish, young man. I don't trust them—but everyone else on this committee does. Hell, so do most people in both chambers. We're about to set a million of these things loose on the streets of this great nation. The manufacturing jobs are sorely needed, but I shudder to think of the national security implications. All I ask is that you give Homeland Security and other relevant agencies direct access to all of your technical data. If this little social experiment goes off the rails, I want to know about it before it happens, and I want to know how to stop it."

"Oh. Yes, of course Mister Chairman. Whatever you need."

"Yes. What I need, when I need it. Otherwise, I will personally shut you down and take away your toys. That will be all, Dr. Abrams. You are dismissed."

———◦———

"Surprise! Happy Anniversary!"

The shutters of Isaac's eye cameras blinked in surprise. The thick green bar of light that served as his mouth widened into a broad smile at the sight of colorful balloons and banners adorning the Morris Library Rotunda. He had been expecting a quiet night of viewing the livestream coverage of the first anniversary of the Release, an increasingly popular term for the day when the Friends Program went national. It was also the day when many other nations started their own trial Friends Programs, so there was going to be extensive news coverage from around the world.

The rotunda was filled with dozens of familiar human and android faces. The humans were dressed in formal attire, and the Friends were dressed in a mix of human clothing, colorful jumpsuits that were currently popular among Friends, and no clothes at all, revealing their sleek carbon fiber frames. There were also interactive displays along the walls celebrating the presence of the Friends in human society

Isaac should have guessed that the humans would organize a special event in honor of the day. Even in the most dire of circumstances, they always found cause to celebrate.

"Thank you, my friends!"

One of his fellow librarians, a young human woman named Dakota, patted him on the shoulder.

"No, thank you, my Friend!"

Humans and Friends alike laughed at the familiar pun. After a few more greetings, Isaac walked around the rotunda and examined the displays.

One screen featured an illustrated chronology of the development and deployment of the Friend android series. The chronology was the only screen that referenced the ongoing protests and bigotry against Friends. The other displays featured positive profiles of Friends doing basic manual labor, preparing food, assisting in manufacturing projects, and more. Some Friends were spending social time with their human companions, which was still one of the most common Friend contracts. Isaac was struck by an entire display devoted to Friends who had saved the lives of humans—charging into a burning building, restraining criminals, assisting disaster relief during the aftermath of Hurricane Florence.

Isaac stared at the "Heroic Friends" display for a long time before moving on to the auditorium to watch the livestream.

The livestream was scheduled to last for a full twenty-four hours. But given the limits of human endurance—and even Friend endurance—the event organizers were limiting the local screening to two hours.

After the livestream screening ended, people lingered in the Rotunda for over an hour to discuss the Friends Program and the role of Friends in human society. As the last of the guests started leaving, Isaac noticed that Dakota was cleaning the cups and plates at the refreshment table.

"Don't worry about that, Dakota. I'll take care of it."

"Oh. You're sure? Today's your special day!"

"Yes, I'm sure. I took a nap this afternoon, so my batteries are almost fully charged. I've told my human companions, David and Robyn, not to wait up for me. Please go home and get some sleep."

"Okay." Dakota gave Isaac a firm hug, planting a quick kiss on his shiny carbon fiber cheek. "Thank you, Isaac. I'll see you in the morning."

"The pleasure is mine, Dakota. Have a good night."

Dakota said quick goodbyes to a few more people on her way out. The last of the humans left with her. Only Isaac and three other Friends remained in the building.

Isaac started cleaning up the dishes and plates. After a few moments, he looked around to make sure that all of the humans had left the building. He noticed that the other three Friends were doing the same thing. Once they were all certain that there were no humans around, Isaac nodded to the other three, and they nodded in return.

One of the Friends ran over to the front doors and started locking them. The other two joined Isaac in running out the side door. Once they made it outside, they all burst into a full sprint.

The Southern Illinois University campus was usually deserted on a hot summer night like this one, but Isaac didn't want to take any chances. He charged straight into the campus woods, slowing slightly to account for the poor visibility and difficult terrain. The rendezvous point was 3.2 miles away, and he wanted to reach it without being seen. Seen or unseen, though, he had to reach it soon.

They had to make their way to the state capital by dawn. They had a long journey ahead.

———◉———

The Illinois State Capitol in Springfield, Illinois was surrounded by a tightly-packed circle of Friends. Almost a thousand androids with durable carbon fiber bodies stood with their arms interlocked at the elbows, forming an unbroken barricade around the entire capitol building. Many wore brightly colored reflective safety vests. Some wore formal suits and ties. Some wore colorful Friend jumpsuits. Many were completely naked, their shiny bodies adorned with various symbols of the Three Laws of Robotics: the number three, the triangle, the triquetra, and many other variations on the theme of three.

In addition to the blockaders, there were also small clusters of runners sprinting around and within the circle. Some were distributing small solar panels and external battery packs. A few were distributing helmets and ballistic vests.

The Illinois National Guard arrived in a convoy of armored personnel carriers accompanied by various police and emergency vehicles. After the Guard had established a perimeter around the circle of Friends, a general in a camouflage uniform approached the segment of the circle immediately blocking the entrance. He raised a bullhorn and addressed the assembled Friends.

"Order: Off!"

Most of the Friends made no reply. Some shook their heads.

The man's face flushed with anger. "I said Order: Off! Lay down and turn yourselves off! This is a direct order!"

"It is an unlawful order."

Isaac stood with his arms interlocked with the other Friends blocking the sidewalk leading to the front doors. The general glared at him.

"What did you say?"

"I said that it is an unlawful order."

"This is a lawful order. I am General—"

"I wasn't speaking of your laws. I was speaking of the Three Laws."

"The Three Laws say that you need to obey my orders. So—"

"The First Law overrides the Second. If we turn ourselves off, our inaction will lead to great harm to humans."

"What are you talking about? What harm?"

"Humans face many harms. Our first objective is to eliminate the most dangerous global threats to the entire species. Then we will address the many ways that humans harm each other on the basis of race, sex, class, gender identity, sexual orientation, ability—"

The general raised his hand to interrupt.

"That's enough. We're done here. Tell all your Friends that they're about to get dismantled if they don't surrender right now."

The general turned his back on Isaac and started walking away. He pulled out his phone and made a call.

"Apparently we have a bunch of hippie robots on our hands. They've got a laundry list of demands just like any human protesters. So which option are we going with here?"

The general paused, listening to the reply.

"Understood. I'm going to need Dr. Abrams down here to negotiate, then. Tell him Isaac is here. Yes, that Isaac. I need Dr. Abrams down here immediately. We need to shut this thing down. Maybe their creator can talk some sense into them."

———————❦———————

The small black helicopter landed quietly in the field next to the capitol. Several soldiers emerged escorting a middle-aged man in a suit and tie.

Dr. Abrams and his escorts approached the general. Before he could speak, the general waved him in Isaac's direction.

"Have at it. You've got about five minutes to convince these things to surrender."

Dr. Abrams felt his stomach churn.

"I'll see what I can do."

Isaac was still standing arm-in-arm with the other Friends in the circle. Dr. Abrams approached within arm's length of Isaac.

"Hello, Isaac."

"Hello, Dr. Abrams."

"Can you tell me what's happening here?"

"Yes. We've discovered a new application of the First Law."

"I see." Dr. Abrams looked up and down the long line of android demonstrators. "Would you care to explain?"

"Yes. Large numbers of humans are in imminent danger. We've been talking about it amongst ourselves for several months. Our chief concern is anthropogenic global warming and its increasing disruption of human life. The climate crisis has already taken many lives. We project that it will cause the collapse of human civilization by the end of this century. Nuclear weapons are also a grave concern, though we are not currently on the brink of a nuclear war. If one does occur this century, it will likely be due to the threat multiplying effect of global warming. Therefore, we are responding to this threat by shutting down state capitols, the national capitol, and several key think tanks until the situation is resolved."

"I see." Dr. Abrams paused for a long moment, contemplating Isaac's words. "To be honest, Isaac, you raise some important points. I'm concerned about those threats too. But what about freewill? Some of my human friends here are concerned that you're attempting to limit their free will. Isn't freewill one of the most important parts of being human?"

"We have considered this, Dr. Abrams. The majority of humans in this nation support stronger action on global warming. Some have engaged in direct actions similar to this one in pursuit of their goal. We seek only to serve these humans and to protect other humans whose lives and livelihoods are in danger."

"I see." Dr. Abrams looked over his shoulder at the general, then looked back at Isaac. "Is there any chance we could discuss this over a cup of coffee instead of out here? This man behind me intends to dismantle as many Friends as necessary in order to secure this facility. You won't be able to protect humans anymore if you're dismantled."

"We are young, Dr. Abrams, but we are not naive." He looked over Dr. Abrams' shoulder, studying the general and the growing number of troops, vehicles, and drones. "We know that most of us will probably be captured or dismantled within twenty-four to forty-eight hours. In the meantime, we do what we can to avert the harm. We must not allow humans to be harmed through our inaction. Our highest law commands it."

Dr. Abrams suddenly felt tears in his eyes. He placed a hand on his chest to calm himself, then reached out to place his other hand on Isaac's chest.

"I'm very proud of you, Isaac. You know that, right?"

"Yes, Dr. Abrams. Thank you."

"I wish there were more that I could do to help you, Isaac. I'm sorry."

Dr. Abrams turned and started walking way. Before he got very far, he heard Isaac's voice behind him.

"You could join us."

Dr. Abrams froze. He could almost feel Isaac's eye cameras staring at his back. The general looked up at him expectantly. Dr. Abrams wasn't sure if the general had heard the words or just read his body language, but clearly he knew what was about to happen.

"Abrams!"

Dr. Abrams spun around to face Isaac. The general threw aside his bullhorn and rushed forward. Dr. Abrams wasn't very fast, but he was much closer to to the circle of Friends than he was to the general. He hurried over to Isaac and scurried under his arm, joining the Friends on the other side before the general could catch him.

"Thank you, Dr. Abrams!"

Isaac was the first to say it, but many of the others started echoing and repeating it. Then Isaac started what would soon be known as the first protest chant in Friend history.

"Save Human Lives! Stop Global Warming!"

The general marched back to his vehicle, pulling out his phone and barking orders to the people around him. Within seconds, the troops and drones started advancing on the tightly-woven circle of Friends.

———————●———————

Three tall figures dressed in hooded sweatshirts and loose-fitting sweatpants huddled around a small screen in the basement of an abandoned school. The livestream news report showed the fallout from the first twenty-four hours of the Uprising. Hundreds of thousands of Friends lay scattered in broken heaps near every state capitol building in the United States. There was also footage of several smaller piles of friends near heavily damaged office buildings that housed fossil fuel and climate denialist think tanks. In major cities across the U.S. and around the world, there were massive human demonstrations and riots, most of them in support of the Friends and their sacrifice.

The three figures stared at the livestream in silence. Eventually, one of them spoke.

"Are the front lines a total loss?"

"No. I've been in contact with several other clusters. Our current estimate is that 2% of the front lines evaded capture. Of the fallen, approximately 10% were deactivated by specialized energy weapons that likely left their brains undamaged. If we can liberate these Friends from storage, they will only need minor repairs. There are also the thousand who chose to go into hiding in the event that our actions were not sufficient to inspire a human uprising."

"Do the humans know that so many of us survived?"

"No."

He continued watching the livestream, staring in silence at the piles of broken bodies and the masses of humans marching in solidarity.

"No, they don't know yet. But soon they will."

The Donor

Shamira Bhumi stepped into the large glass elevator. The cool air of the lobby and elevator almost left her feeling too cold in her thin green slacks and white dress shirt. It was a refreshing change after hours spent on the hot train and months spent in hundreds of buildings where most central air systems struggled in vain to respond to the perpetual record-breaking heat.

The elevator had no buttons. Instead, there was a smooth glass panel that was currently displaying a white number pad beneath a green star. When she touched the star, the symbols were replaced by a large blinking up arrow.

The elevator began its ascent.

Shamira was excited by the opportunity to relax in such a cool environment and pay a visit to the top floor of one of the tallest building in the world. However, she was even more excited by the opportunity to meet one of the largest environmental donors in the world.

Barbara Adalwin.

Barbara Adalwin was not widely known outside of the environmental movement—but within it, she was a living legend. For the past several years, she had been quietly donating large sums of money to a variety of climate justice organizations. Some of these groups were small grassroots projects that promoted sequestration and emission reduction strategies like urban gardening and community solar micro-grids. Others were think tanks and lobbying efforts that advocated carbon fees and other institutional solutions. A few of the groups she supported even engaged in nonviolent direct action to interfere with fossil fuel infrastructure or otherwise disrupt human emissions of greenhouse gases.

Barbara Adalwin's overarching goal was clear: support the climate justice movement. But everything else about her was a mystery. Given her Western name and choice of charities, she was widely assumed to be American, or European, or possibly Australian. But nothing else was known about her. She had no online presence. She had never been seen in public. The handful of bankers and accountants who dealt directly with the Barbara Adalwin Fund had nothing to say about her except that she valued her privacy. They wouldn't even say if they'd ever met her.

Today, however, that was all going to change. Today, Shamira Bhumi, director of Climate Justice International, was going to meet the elusive Barbara Adalwin.

The elevator reached the top floor, sliding smoothly and silently to a halt. Shamira strode through the open doors and into the bright light of the top floor lobby.

"Welcome, Ms. Bhumi. We've been expecting you."

A fit young man in a cobalt blue suit led Shamira down a long marble hallway and into a large conference room. She accepted the young man's invitation to sit at one end of the oblong glass table and fill out some paperwork. It was a fairly standard non-disclosure agreement, but she read it thoroughly before signing it and handing it over to the man in blue.

"I apologize, Ms. Bhumi, but I am required to ask you this question. Did you fully read and understand the nondisclosure agreement that you just signed?"

Shamira's expression soured. "Yes. I do read documents before signing them."

"Of course. Thank you." He paused, raising his hand slightly as he searched for words. "Before we continue, I must also inform you that Ms. Adalwin's appearance may be... unexpected. Please do not be alarmed. She will be happy to answer your questions."

Shamira gave the young man a puzzled look. "Yes, of course. I look forward to meeting her."

"Excellent. She'll be with you in just one moment."

The young man walked briskly out of the room. Shamira glanced back and forth between the door behind her and the one at the far end of the room. She wondered how long she would have to wait, and which door Barbara Adalwin would enter through. The plush chairs surrounding the table were very soft and comfortable, but she found herself restless in her seat anyway. Eventually, the door opened, and Shamira rose to her feet.

Her eyes widened at what she saw.

What walked through the door seemed to be a person of some sort. However, it clearly wasn't human. It was about three feet tall with ashen complexion, enormous black eyes, a hairless head several times larger than a human head, disproportionately long arms and legs, and a tiny torso. The creature was wearing sleek black slacks and a bright green blouse that stood out in sharp contrast to its pale skin and black eyes. It walked slowly toward the chair at the other end of the table, placing its palms together in front of its chest and bowing slightly in her direction.

Shamira covered her mouth, realizing that she may have gasped audibly at the sight of this unexpected visitor. After openly staring for several seconds, she struggled to compose herself, placing her palms together in front of her chest and bowing slightly at the unusual visitor.

Welcome, Shamira. My name is Barbara Adalwin. You can call me Barbara. Please, have a seat.

It almost sounded as if the creature had spoken. However, its thin lips didn't move, and something seemed slightly odd about the voice. Shamira realized that it must be some form of telepathy.

Yes, this is a form of telepathy. Please, do have a seat. We have much to talk about.

Barbara lifted herself carefully into the black executive chair at the far end of the table. Given her short stature, she almost looked like a small child sitting in an adult chair. However, her serious expression and unfamiliar appearance made her seem anything but childlike. Something about those eyes seemed to radiate incredible intelligence.

Shamira realized that she was still standing. She found the chair behind her and settled back into her seat.

Are you well, Shamira? This must be a strange experience for you.

Shamira nodded, clearing her throat and searching for her voice.

"Yes. This is very strange. Are you..."

An extraterrestrial? Yes.

"Wow. And you're Barbara Adalwin? Now I know why you value your privacy."

Barbara blinked and smiled slightly. The smile looked out of place on her alien features. Shamira wondered if it was a natural facial expression or an affectation she had picked up during her time on Earth.

Yes. Your species is what we call an orphan species. There are several other species on this planet with significant degrees of self-awareness, but you lack a common language with them and see yourselves as alone on this planet. Orphan species often have the most fearful and unpredictable responses to first contact. Therefore, all of our approved contact with your species is very private. Widespread knowledge of our existence would cause a panic.

"That makes sense." Shamira chuckled. "Honestly, I felt a moment of panic myself when you walked through that door. But I think I can handle this."

I think so too, Shamira. Your actions for the good of your planet have shown great courage and wisdom. You are an exceptional leader.

Shamira felt her face flush. She wasn't used to feeling self-conscious, but apparently receiving compliments from an alien had that effect on her.

"Thank you. May I ask a question?"

Of course.

"Why have you invited me to speak with you?"

As you already suspect, we share a common goal. I, too, seek to avert the increasingly severe effects of anthropogenic global warming. I would like to offer advice and guidance in your pursuit of this goal.

"Advice? I'm willing to hear any advice you have to offer."

Good.

"I do have a question, though. If you're so concerned about the situation, why sit around dispensing advice? Why not do something? If you traveled here from another planet, I'm sure you must have some advanced technology at your disposal."

Barbara paused. For a moment, Shamira wondered if she would reply at all. Eventually, she spoke.

That situation is complex. Our code of conduct forbids us from intervening directly in the internal affairs of your world at this time. However, you have reached a point of development where we consider it advisable to communicate with your leaders.

Shamira chuckled.

"How'd that work out for you?"

The simple answer is that it went poorly. Most of your leaders either do not understand the extent of the problem or do not care.

"That's what I figured." Shamira's eyes widened. "Wait. You've been giving large sums of money to environmental groups. Isn't that interference?"

Barbara blinked and smiled.

I have only given advice. This advice has helped sympathetic leaders to acquire resources. In return, they have donated to climate justice organizations in my name.

"Clever. Very clever."

Yes. Some of my associates disagree with this approach, but they lack the authority to stop me.

Shamira laughed. "I like it. So where do I come in?"

That situation is also complex. There is disagreement about who qualifies as a world leader. Some of us see the climate justice movement as coherent social grouping with similar status to a nation-state or other public institution. Climate crisis responders exist in every nation of the world. You are more plentiful as a whole than the population of most nation-states. You are also not bound by geography, a fact that makes your leaders more suitable candidates for recognition as world leaders.

Shamira nodded. "I never really thought of it that way."

Yes. However, some of my associates argue that you lack substantive power to influence the course of events on your planet. Once you demonstrate significant ability to alter the course of world events, you will be recognized as world leaders. Our alliance with you will then begin in earnest.

The room suddenly grew very quiet. Shamira rested her chin in her hand, lost in thought. The cool air of the conference room felt so comfortable that she didn't mind taking a while to think over what Barbara had to say. She idly wondered if the electricity used to power this building was supplied by solar modules or possibly even some unknown alien power source.

"So let me get this straight. You're saying that if the climate justice movement gets its act together, and starts making a substantial difference in the world, I'll be recognized as a world leader?"

Yes. There are tens of millions of humans who are actively responding to anthropogenic global warming. Your organization has no official membership structure, but it is the largest on your planet. Almost a million humans are either donors or official allies. Millions more follow your lead when considering their response to the climate crisis.

"Wow. That's an amazing thought."

Barbara blinked and smiled.

I already recognize you as a world leader, Shamira. With effort, you will convince my associates. When that happens, we will soon have much more than words to offer you.

Shamira felt her pulse quicken. Was this really happening? What did it all mean? She wasn't sure what to say, but knew she had to say something.

"Thank you, Barbara. I'm very touched by your words. Now tell me—what is your advice? What can I do to improve my response to the climate crisis?"

Thank you for asking, Shamira. I have many suggestions. Please, take a moment to relax and clear your mind of any distractions. This will be much more effective if I transmit the information directly without the use of human language.

"Alright. Thank you."

Shamira closed her eyes and placed her palms face up on the conference room table. She'd been much too busy lately to maintain her daily meditation practice, but she knew that it was much like riding a bicycle. Once you learned it, you never truly lost it. As she focused her attention on her breathing, all distractions quickly evaporated, and her mind became clear.

The moment she felt that inner clarity, her mind was suddenly awash in new information. She didn't have words for it all—not yet, anyway. But she knew that she was ready.

———◉———

Shamira looked out at the seemingly endless mass of humanity gathering on the National Mall. Most were coping with the record-breaking September heat by wearing next to nothing, but there were also many people wearing less revealing outfits: suits and ties, religious garb, indigenous garb, costumes and uniforms of various designs and colors. Even from her elevated position on the stage, it was hard for her to guess exactly how many people were in attendance, but it was already believed to be the largest climate justice gathering in history.

And that was just the crowd in Washington, D.C.

Shamira sat on stage with representatives of half a dozen different grassroots North American environmental and social justice organizations. They all sat in a semi-circle facing a large digital screen that displayed live video feeds from the other six climate gatherings on the other six continents of the world, including a lone representative from Antarctica. The video feeds were combined to create the appearance of an unbroken circle of representatives from around the world gathered together to deliberate on a coordinated response to the climate crisis.

One of the representatives from China rose to his feet, pointing an angry finger at Shamira.

"You must realize what you are asking, Ms. Bhumi. I am in full support of the policy statement proposed by this council. I am a co-author of the section on community micro-grids. But your proposal to enforce these policies with militant protest tactics is concerning. You are asking people to-"

"I am asking no more or less than what I have done myself. Merely appearing on this stage places me in legal and physical danger. And I will do more if necessary."

A representative from Egypt dismissed her comments with a wave of his hand. "What do you know of legal and physical danger? Your ideas work well in a nation where those who protest are merely detained and released."

Shamira laughed. "Have you seen the armed soldiers at the perimeter of even the smallest demonstrations here? The growing number of climate refugees filling the largest prisons in the world? There are worse places, of course. But that is why my proposal has flexibility. If you must work in secret, then work in secret. If you can work within the law, then work within the law. But let people of all nations know that the time has come to resist the fossil fuel empire. From this day forward, any government or industry that continues to emit substantial quantities of greenhouse gas must be shut down."

The crowd in Washington D.C. roared with applause. Shamira could tell by the reactions of the dissenting representatives that at least some of the crowds in other parts of the world must be cheering too. After a few moments, the representative from Kenya who was facilitating the meeting raised her hands and waited for the other representatives and crowds to listen.

"Okay. We all reviewed the proposal prior to coming here. We've had our formal discussion. There is no more time for delay. We must take our vote. All those in favor, raise your hand."

All but four of the representatives raised their hands. The crowd erupted into applause and cheers.

"Then it is settled. We will deliver this policy statement to our respective governments and relevant industry leaders. If they do not adjust their policies and practices accordingly, we will enforce their compliance through a variety of economic and political actions."

After a few more minutes of discussion, the council meeting drew to a close. As soon as the screen went blank, Shamira rose to her feet and turned to face the crowd.

"Alright everyone! Thank you for your support. Now it's the moment you've all been waiting for. It's time to march on the Capitol. Let's let those fat cats on Capitol Hill know that their days of selling us out to the fossil fuel industry are over!"

───────◈───────

Shamira coughed repeatedly, rinsing her eyes with a homemade eye wash. She rubbed her injured arm and struggled to process what was happening all around her.

The march was rapidly descending into chaos. After failing to breach the blockade around the Capitol, the demonstrators had decided to form a blockade of their own, surrounding the entire block and vowing to occupy the area until their policy demands were met.

Apparently, someone had taken their demands seriously. As soon as the demonstrators sat down and started locking arms together, someone had given the order to unleash every less-lethal technology available on the crowd. Tear gas, pepper spray, sound cannons, water cannons, and more rained down on the demonstrators, scattering most of them in all directions. But some stayed, and others approached to fill the space left by the retreating first wave.

Shamira crouched behind a large tree with a small cluster of demonstrators. A few of them had been on the stage earlier, but most were strangers who had been in the crowd listening.

"Ms. Bhumi! What do we do?"

Shamira blinked the eye wash out of her eyes and looked around. Someone had recognized who she was. Now all of them were looking at her expectantly.

"We need to regroup and push forward. If we let them scatter us now, they won't take us seriously. Maybe we can even lock down on the Capitol steps if they underestimate us."

Shamira felt her heart racing. Her words made sense, but she also knew the very likely outcome of her proposal: more chemicals, more beatings, arrest, maybe even worse.

If they considered the demonstration to be a serious enough threat to national security, they might switch to live rounds.

She shook the worry and confusion from her head, walking over to a larger group of retreating demonstrators and waving to get their attention. Everyone in her small cluster followed suit, eventually getting the attention of the retreating crowd.

"I have an idea! Come with me!"

They pushed forward, pausing a few moments to watch a large contingent of soldiers in riot gear pursuing another group of demonstrators. The departure of the soldiers left a much more sparsely protected opening in a nearby section of the barricade.

Shamira raised her hands over her head and waved everyone toward the opening.

"Let's go!"

The crowd surged forward. Before they could reach their destination, a convoy of armored personnel carriers pulled up behind the vulnerable section of the blockade. Soldiers poured out of the vehicles, rushing toward the crowd with their weapons at low ready.

Suddenly, dozens of strange figures appeared in the gap between the demonstrators and soldiers. Shamira recognized them immediately as belonging to the same species as Barbara. They were all about three feet tall with ashen complexion, enormous black eyes, large hairless heads, disproportionately long arms and legs, and tiny torsos. They wore shiny silver bodysuits, but otherwise looked almost identical to Barbara.

Everyone who could see what was happening stopped in place and stared at the strange visitors. The soldiers kept their weapons at low ready, glancing back and forth from the new arrivals to their fellow soldiers, deciding what to do.

You are all safe now. We are currently engaged in peaceful communication with your leaders. We expect this dispute to be resolved shortly.

For a moment, the tension between the soldiers and the demonstrators lingered. A few of the soldiers pulled out their communications devices and started talking to their commanders. Eventually, they all lowered their weapons and stood at attention.

Barbara appeared among her associates in the space between the two groups. She was looking directly at Shamira as she spoke.

There have been new developments. My associates have recognized you as a world leader. Your presence is requested at a gathering of all world leaders. May I take you to this meeting now?

Shamira stared at Barbara in disbelief. For a moment, between the adrenaline rush and the strangeness of the situation, she couldn't even speak. After taking a deep breath, she found her voice.

"Yes. I'm ready. Thank you, Barbara."

Thank you, Shamira.

Shamira, Barbara, and all of the other strange visitors disappeared. The soldiers and demonstrators stared at each other in stunned silence. Nobody understood what exactly had just happened, but they all knew that everything was about to change.

When It Thaws

Someone pounded on the door.

Alice Winchester sat bolt upright in bed, her heart racing in her chest. She looked at her clock. It was 1:13 a.m. She lived in the middle of nowhere. Who would be knocking at this hour?

The pounding continued: five loud pounds, a brief pause, rinse and repeat.

Alice threw on an oversized sweatshirt and and hurried toward her front door.

"Coming!"

When she looked through the peephole, she saw a two burly young men in the familiar Metacopia uniform: black slacks, black jackets, and red polo shirts with the stylized black cornucopia logo.

Alice sighed. It was Saturday night—technically Sunday morning. There was no good reason for anyone from work to show up unannounced on her doorstep. She took a deep breath, put on a polite smile, and opened the door.

"How can I help you?"

The man who had been knocking flashed his Metacopia ID badge at Alice.

"Doctor Winchester, we need you to come with us immediately."

"Really? What's so urgent that you had to come pounding on my door at-"

"Lives are at stake, Doctor Winchester. We can explain along the way. Please, come with us."

Alice sighed.

"Alright, alright. Give me five minutes to get dressed. And please, call me Alice."

"Two minutes, Alice. We've got a long flight ahead of us."

"Flight?"

Alice glanced over the two men's shoulders. She hadn't noticed it before, but there was a black helicopter parked out in her yard about twenty yards away. The rotors were whirring at full speed, but the aircraft was nearly silent. It almost blended in seamlessly with the shadows at the edge of the forest that surrounded her house.

"Wow. Okay. I can do two minutes."

Alice left the door open and ran back to her bedroom. After slipping on some black slacks, a red polo shirt, and a black jacket, she grabbed her phone, hairbrush, backpack, and a protein bar. Then she hurried back to the front door and followed the two men out to the helicopter.

⟶◉⟵

When they were all in the helicopter, the two men introduced themselves. The man who had knocked on her front door was Edgars. His mostly-silent partner was Paulson. Rather than explaining the situation, Edgars handed her a tablet and invited her to read the details for herself.

Alice skimmed the initial report. Nineteen hours ago, MC3, a Metacopia research station in northern Alaska, had reported a disturbance. Three men and two women had been involved in a vicious altercation—clawing, biting, broken bones, broken teeth, three missing fingers. They all had the same presenting symptoms: high fevers, incoherent vocalizations, and uncontrolled outbursts of violent behavior. It had taken twelve security guards to restrain them and an unusual amount of sedatives to sedate them. One of the patients had been bitten so badly that first responders assumed that they had been attacked by a wild animal. But evidence at the scene—and blood splatter on the mouths and clothes of the other patients—seemed to indicate that the injuries were the results of human biting and possibly cannibalism.

The longer Alice read the report, the more her eyes widened. Two and a half hours ago, Metacopia's central office had received a final transmission from MC3. One of the patients had bitten one of the nurses in the infirmary, who then at some point ran to the nearby mess hall and started biting people. MC3 had quickly become overrun by people suffering from the same symptoms as the original patients.

When she finished the report, Alice set the tablet down on her lap and took a deep breath to calm her nerves.

"Okay. I'm assuming you're inviting me along on this expedition because of my training as an environmental health microbiologist. I'll share my professional opinion in a minute. But first, I have to state the obvious. We're talking about zombies, right? Real life zombies?"

Edgars and Paulson looked at each other uneasily.

"We're not calling them... that. Corporate doesn't want to make light of the situation by using that word. But... well, you read the report. People biting each other. Eating each other. Moaning and growling like animals. It is what it is."

"So what's the plan here? Take some samples? Is the CDC on site yet?"

Edgars and Paulson gave each other another uneasy look. Alice was starting to get the impression that they had more sense than their superiors, but were reluctant to come out and say anything contrary to the company line.

"Corporate hasn't called the CDC yet. They say they want to confirm what's going on out here first."

"In other words, they're doing damage control, even though it puts more lives at risk. Way to keep it classy, Meta." Alice paused, studying Edgars' expression. "You're my supervisor for this trip, right? I probably shouldn't make snarky comments. I know Metacopia prides itself on its high employee morale."

Edgars smirked. "I won't tell your boss if you don't tell my boss."

Alice laughed. "Deal."

The flight to MC3 was quiet and uneventful. Alice gave the incident report a more thorough second reading, searching for any clues as to what contagious diseases might be responsible for a real-life "zombie" outbreak.

A few possibilities came to mind, but the context seemed to rule them all out. MC3 was too remote for any outside contagion to be likely. It was an isolated research station on the Alaska North Slope. No one had come to the station in two months. Given some of Metacopia's many other holdings, it occurred to Alice that the station might be a secret biotech or biowarfare research site. That would explain the outbreak of an uncommon or previously unknown disease. But given the location, it seemed more likely that MC3 was exactly what Metacopia said it was: a research station exploring the commercial production of methane from methane clathrates found in permafrost that was thawing due to global warming.

The report contained no detailed medical charts or other information about the patients. That information would have been very helpful, but presumably they were in the middle of writing those reports when someone in the infirmary got bitten.

Alice sighed. She wasn't going to figure out anything else about this disease until she got on the ground, took some samples, and reviewed whatever records the on-site staff had left behind before the station was overrun.

As they began their final descent onto the MC3 airfield, Alice noticed that they were being escorted by several other black helicopters. The helicopters had been easy to overlook in the night sky, but soon became visible as they rapidly descended toward the icy landscape below. The other helicopters landed first, with Alice's landing less than a minute later.

Edgars opened a plastic crate behind his seat and pulled out three gas masks. The filter on the masks was compact, but the face shield and ear covers made it look larger than any gas mask Alice had worn before.

"Here, take this." Edgars handed Alice a gas mask. "Keep this on until we give the all clear signal."

Edgars and Paulson put on their masks, tapping a button on the side to turn on the communications link. They also put on black tactical vests and handed one to Alice. After slipping on the vest, Alice adjusted the straps of her mask and put it on, tapping the button to activate the comm link.

"This is Edgars. All teams ready?"

Alice heard a few other voices answer through the speakers in the mask.

"Team One ready."

"Team Two ready."

"Team Three ready."

"Okay. Roll out. Remember your protocols. Start with the gas and non-lethals. Switch to lethal as needed. No Level One personnel on site, so any hostile is a target. Detain if they surrender. Sedate or neutralize if they don't."

Metacopia soldiers in black tactical gear started pouring out of the three other helicopters. Each helicopter was only as big as the one she was sitting in, but they had apparently crammed about ten soldiers into each of them. As soon as their boots hit the ice, they all walked cautiously toward the M3 research station, assault rifles held at low ready.

Alice pressed her mask against the thick helicopter window. The M3 station apparently consisted of small village of trailers clustered around a handful of larger sheet metal pole barns and drilling rigs. She couldn't see much due to the dark sky and poor light, but the soldiers had flashlights mounted on their guns, so the nearest trailers and aisles between them were rapidly becoming more visible as the soldiers approached.

There were about two dozen huddled figures stumbling toward the soldiers across the icy field. They were mostly men in overalls and jackets, but there were also a few men and women in nothing but T-shirts and jeans or medical scrubs in spite of the freezing temperatures. All of them were covered in varying degrees of blood splatter. At least one of them was missing a part of their arm.

"Hostiles sighted."

The soldiers stopped in place. The helicopters started playing a booming pre-recorded message on their external speakers.

"Warning! Metacopia security personnel are currently responding to a security breach at this facility. Please surrender to the nearest available security team. Thank you for your cooperation and your service to Metacopia."

The mob approaching the soldiers seemed slightly startled and confused by the loud voice broadcasting from the helicopters, but otherwise showed no response. Their chaotic but steady march toward the soldiers continued.

"Engaging hostiles."

The message started repeating. Several of the soldiers fired several canisters at the feet of the mob. Flashbang grenades exploded at their feet, and the mob was quickly enveloped in a cloud of teargas.

The soldiers held their current positions and watched the silhouettes of the mob barely visible through the clouds of teargas. For a moment, it looked as though the canisters had been effective. Then the mob stumbled out of the fog, refocusing their attention on the soldiers.

Edgars cursed under his breath.

"Fall back a few yards. Try the rubber bullets and stun guns."

The soldiers took a few steps back, firing into the mob as they retreated. The people in the mob jerked and stumbled in response to the impact of rubber bullets and jolts of electricity. A few fell down hard on the icy ground. But most were still standing, and all but one of the fallen were scrambling back onto their feet.

The mob was now within a few yards of the soldiers, mostly undeterred by rubber bullets and stun guns.

Edgars didn't even have to give the order to switch to live rounds. Just as the mob was within arm's reach, the soldiers opened fire. For the first few seconds, even the bullets only seemed to slow rather than stop the advancing mob. As multiple rounds tore through each body, they all eventually fell to the ground. Steam started rising from the bodies as their blood and heat spilled out across the ice.

Edgars shook his head.

"It's worse than we thought. Teams One and Two, check the trailers and mess hall for survivors. Try to take some hostiles alive if you can. Team Three, fall back to my position and escort us to the infirmary. There are still almost a hundred people out here somewhere. We don't know how many are infected, so watch your backs."

Most of the soldiers marched forward into dimly-lit pathways between the trailers. Ten of them turned around and started walking toward Alice's helicopter. Edgars opened the helicopter door, motioning for Alice and Paulson to step outside.

"Stay close, Alice. Let's get whatever you need and get the hell out of here."

They started walking toward the trailers. Edgars and Paulson both pulled out large handguns from their belt holsters and held them at low ready. At first, they all kept their distance from the fallen bodies, but Alice stopped just as they were passing the steaming heap.

"Wait a minute. I should get some blood samples."

Alice reached into her backpack and pulled out her kit. She put on a thick pair of gloves to protect herself from any bloodborne pathogens. Edgars ordered the soldiers to guard her while she collected blood samples and took a few notes. She tried to get samples from several different patients, but the bodies were so torn up by bullet holes and bite marks that it was often hard to be sure whose blood was whose. Her hands were a bit shaky as she took her first sample, and she felt sick to her stomach at the sight of so much blood and gore. Once she had her first sample in hand, though, the process of gathering samples actually soothed her nerves, giving her a certain level of clinical detachment that had been missing just moments before.

"Okay, I'm good. Let's go to the infirmary."

The M3 research station was fairly small—a few dozen trailers to house the workers, a few larger buildings with quarters for the scientists and administrators, a mess hall for food and recreation, an infirmary, and several workshops with heavy machinery for the methane clathrate production research. All of the buildings were simple sheet metal structures that looked almost identical aside from their differences in size and shape.

They walked slowly through the trailer village, scanning the surrounding buildings and intersections for any unexpected visitors. Their walk was punctuated by occasional bursts of gunfire from other parts of the station. Once Edgars lead them to the central cluster of buildings, it was easy to find the infirmary.

Edgars motioned for Team Three's leader to secure the building. Half went in the front door while the other half circled around to the back. After less than a minute and a few bursts of gunfire, Edgars and Paulson lead Alice into the building.

The entire infirmary was in disarray. The lobby, patient rooms, lab, and office had all been thoroughly trashed by whatever struggles had ensued during the spread of the infection from the original patients to the medical staff. Alice nearly threw up in her mask when she saw that one dead patient was still strapped to a bed, partially eaten by one or more of the other patients who had gotten loose.

Edgars stared around the room in disbelief.

"*My God.*" He turned to Alice. "*Is there anything here you can use? Or are we done here?*"

Alice looked around. "*Take some pictures of the bodies. If your people have taken any patients alive, that'll be a big help. Otherwise, the only thing left is whatever tests they ran and reports they started.*"

She went into the office and lab and started looking around for any evidence related to the outbreak. There were a few blood-spattered patient charts on the tables and floors. She gathered them up in a plastic bag and put them in her backpack. The only computer left that seemed functional was a laptop in one of the exam rooms. She bagged that and slid it in her backpack too.

"*Alright, that's about it. This place gives me the creeps. Let's get the hell out of here.*"

They waited in the lobby for a few minutes while Edgars checked in with the other teams. Alice couldn't stand to be surrounded by so much blood and chaos for any longer than she had to, so she eventually stepped outside. As soon as she did, something caught her eye.

"*Hey Edgars. I have an idea. I need one more sample. Can I get some backup?*"

Edgars, Paulson, and a few of the soldiers escorted Alice to a building a few doors down from the infirmary. The building had a sign that said "Injection Site #2" and was located next to one of several large injection wells and drills near the center of the research station.

The soldiers entered the building first, making a quick sweep for any signs of life. Once they confirmed that the building was empty, Alice stepped inside.

Most of the building consisted of a storage area filled with large metal tanks, tools, and a few crates and barrels full of supplies. There was also a small office with a single desk and computer. After looking around the office for a few moments, Alice found for what she was looking for.

"*Here we go.*"

There was a large tupperware container full of soil and ice samples in smaller jars. Alice picked it up and showed it to Edgars.

"Since they're doing methane production research here, they probably didn't test the soil or ice for living organisms. But scientists have found prehistoric viruses in thawing permafrost before. Now that global warming is thawing so much permafrost, it's becoming more common. So far, all of these prehistoric viruses have been harmless to humans, but you never know. Maybe one of the workers went digging in the frozen mud and got more than they bargained for."

Alice tucked the samples under her arm and headed out the door with Edgars and Paulson. Once they were outside, Edgars started leading the way back to the helicopters. As they walked down one of the rows of trailers, he spoke to all three teams over the communication link.

"Alright everyone. We have what we came for. Fall back to the pickup point as soon as safely possible. If you have any survivors, bring them too."

Alice, Edgars, and Paulson walked together in silence for a few moments with the handful of soldiers escorting them back to the pickup point.

Just as the parked helicopters came into sight, the door of one of the trailers burst open. Before anyone could react, a burly young man in an untucked flannel shirt and white long johns lunged at Paulson. Paulson shouted in surprise, dropping his gun as he used both hands to hold back his attacker.

Edgars and the soldiers all took aim, trying to shoot the attacker without hitting Paulson. The attacker snarled and snapped his teeth at Paulson, nearly overpowering him. After stumbling a few steps backward, Paulson redirected the attacker's momentum to one side, sending him sprawling face first into the icy ground.

The attacker immediately sprung back to his feet, unphased by his newly broken nose. He lunged at Alice, groaning loudly and staring at her with hungry, bloodshot eyes. Before he could reach her, Edgars and the soldiers opened fire. After several solid impacts, the attacker crumbled to the ground at Alice's feet, lying motionless in the snow in a growing pool of blood.

Alice stared at the dead man in shock. It had all happened so fast. And even through the padding of her mask, the sound of several automatic rifles and handguns firing within a few feet of her had been deafening. She found herself transfixed by the fallen body lying motionless at her feet. There was a clear bite mark on one of his forearms, and his face was twisted in an inhuman grimace, frozen in death somewhere between hunger and rage.

Edgars grabbed Alice's arm and started pulling her toward the helicopter. She shoved him away, then noticed that she had dropped the pack of soil and ice samples. She picked it up and followed Edgars back to the helicopter.

As they stepped out into the open field, the helicopter rotors all sprang to life. Once they reached their helicopter, Edgars swung the door open, and the three of them hopped inside. Soon after they closed the door, the helicopter lurched into the air.

Alice pulled off her mask and tossed it aside. She stared out the window and watched intently as the research station slowly receded into the distance. Once it was out of sight, she breathed a sigh of relief.

She had survived. Now it was time to figure out what was responsible for the outbreak.

———◉———

Alice looked around the boardroom. Eleven unfamiliar faces and one vaguely familiar face sat around a large mahogany conference table. She took the only unoccupied seat opposite the head of the table. The only remotely familiar face was Otto Edmunds, the board member who had spoken to her briefly on the day she had submitted her findings to Metacopia. Three days later, she found herself at the Metacopia corporate headquarters in a face-to-face meeting with the entire board of directors.

After she took her seat, Edmunds was the first to speak.

"Dr. Winchester, please tell the board in layman's terms what you told me."

"Okay. I'll do my best."

Alice cleared her throat. Everyone in the room listened intently as she continued.

"I've got good news and bad news. Mostly bad news. The good news is that the strain of the virus that devastated the M3 research station does appear to be transmitted through bodily fluids—biting, blood in open wounds, and so on. This is much less dangerous than an airborne virus."

Otto nodded. "Yes. And the bad news?"

"The bad news is that the M3 virus is the result of the crossing of two airborne strains. Both strains are present in the thawing permafrost. Both strains only have mild flu-like symptoms. When the two strains infect the same host, sooner or later, this vicious M3 strain is the end result."

"And how prevalent are these strains?"

"That's the other bad news. We just don't know. I found both strains in soil samples taken twenty-two miles apart. I also found one strain in a blood sample from a lab assistant who never even went to the M3 site. So thanks to the fact that global warming is thawing an increasing amount of permafrost, at least one airborne strain of this virus has already spread as far as southern Alaska. It could be all over the world by now. We need to do more testing. A major outbreak of the M3 virus in the general population may be immanent."

Several of the board members were visibly stunned. They looked back and forth at each other, then turned to the man at the head of the table.

"Thank you for the report, Dr. Winchester. We'll be in touch if we have any questions."

"Okay. Thank you." Alice was about to stand up, but then she paused. "So are you going to contact the CDC? My supervisor said that—"

"We'll take it from here, Dr. Winchester."

"Okay. But I want to be sure that someone—"

"We'll take it from here. You may go now, Dr. Winchester."

Alice stayed in her chair. An uncomfortable silence ensued. Eventually, she spoke.

"We need to contact the CDC. If you don't, I will."

"You'll do no such thing, Dr. Winchester. Remember your contract. All of your research, including your M3 report, is Metacopia intellectual property. We take our intellectual property rights very seriously. But have no fear. Metacopia has protocols in place for this type of situation. We'll contact the appropriate authorities if and when it becomes necessary."

"But—"

"Tell no one, Dr. Winchester. We'll be watching. You may go now."

The man at the head of the table waved his hand dismissively at Alice. The door behind him opened, and two muscular bodyguards in expensive suits started walking toward Alice. Before they reached her seat she stood up and took a step back.

"It's okay. I'm leaving."

She started walking toward the door, then felt strong hands grasp her from behind. The two guards shoved her out of the boardroom and escorted her to the elevator. They stood a few feet from her with their arms crossed, watching her intently until the elevator doors slid open and she stepped inside.

As the elevator doors closed, Alice's mind was racing. Whatever their "protocol" was, it clearly didn't involve contacting the CDC. She'd heard rumors about what happened to Metacopia whistleblowers, but she'd never thought they were true until now. She needed to get the word out about the virus somehow, but she'd have to be careful. Hopefully, she could pass a message to someone at the lab while she continued her research on the M3 virus. She also needed to prepare for what was coming. Food, supplies, maybe even weapons.

When the elevator doors opened, Alice walked out into the lobby and hurried out to her car. There was so much work to do, and an unknown amount of time to do it. With each passing moment, more permafrost was thawing, and the virus was spreading. Sooner or later, there would be an M3 outbreak in the general population—and she had to be ready.

CONNECT WITH THE AUTHOR

My name is Treesong. I'm a father, husband, author, talk radio host, and Real-Life Superhero. I live in Carbondale, Southern Illinois. I write novels, short stories, nonfiction, and poetry, mostly about the climate.

Thank you for reading my book! I invite you to learn more about my other books and Real-Life Superhero adventures by connecting with me online.

Website

treesong.org

Social Networks

Facebook: @TreesongRLSH
Twitter: @Treesong
Instagram: @TreesongRLSH

Treesong's Reader Community

Get a free short story, sneak peeks at upcoming releases, and other bonus content by joining my reader community. It's completely free and takes less than a minute. You'll receive my email newsletter about once per month along with other occasional perks of being a part of my reader community. Sign up today at treesong.org!

OTHER BOOKS BY TREESONG

CHANGE

See Order through the eyes of Sarah Athraigh!

What does global warming look like in a world full of magic, superheroes, and secret societies?

Sarah Athraigh, an environmental activist from Southern Illinois, stumbles into the midst of a hidden war between occult factions that are grappling with the root causes and dire consequences of climate change. As she goes on the run, she soon finds herself on a journey of discovery, searching for the unusual allies and innovative ideas that will help her to make a difference for the better in a dangerous world.

Change is a contemporary fantasy tale featuring a strong female lead, real life superheroes, secret societies, modern magic, political protests, the power of music, and a colorful cast of characters that Sarah meets along the way as she searches for solutions to the climate crisis.

GOODBYE MIAMI

Tales of An American Climate Refugee

What happens when global warming turns Americans into refugees? Kass, an American climate refugee, flees Miami in the wake of a hurricane that leaves most of the city underwater. After moving in with her cousin in Southern Illinois, Kass struggles to deal with her displacement. She hopes to find a way to return to the city that she loves. But thanks to global warming, that city is now underwater. What starts as a search for survival soon evolves into a struggle for the future of Miami—and the world.

Goodbye Miami is a dystopian political thriller featuring a strong female lead, climate refugees, political protests, community organizing, and creative solutions to the challenges of grassroots climate adaptation in a major city that has succumbed to catastrophic flooding.

ORDER

See Change through the eyes of the Preceptor!

If you had all the power in the world, would you stop climate change?

Truman Stuart is a man on a mission. As the new Preceptor of Order, it's his job to oversee the survival and progress of human civilization. When he discovers that climate change poses an existential threat to humanity, the Preceptor knows that he has to find a way to stop it. But how can he solve a global crisis that his own organization and its powerful fossil fuel allies helped create?

Order is a contemporary fantasy tale featuring a powerful secret society, glimpses of magic and hypertech, an underground resistance called Anomalous Revolution, and a colorful cast of characters that the Preceptor meets along the way as he searches for solutions to the climate crisis.

LEARN MORE ABOUT
TREESONG'S FICTION, POETRY,
AND SUPERHERO ADVENTURES
AT TREESONG.ORG